# SUNNY

## JASON REYNOLDS

## Also by Jason Reynolds

Ghost (in the same series)
Patina (in the same series)

Look Both Ways
For Every One
Long Way Down (Faber)
Boy in the Black Suit (Faber)

# SUNNY

## Run: Book 3

# JASON REYNOLDS

Published by Knights Of
Knights Of Ltd, Registered Offices:
119 Marylebone Road, London, NW1 5PU

www.knightsof.media
First published 2019
001

Written by Jason Reynolds
Text and cover copyright © Jason Reynolds, 2019
Cover art by © Selom Sunu, 2019
First published in the USA by Atheneum,
an imprint of Simon and Schuster, Inc, 2018
All rights reserved
The moral right of the author and illustrator has been asserted

Set in ITC Stone Serif / 12 pt
Typeset design by Marssaié Jordan
Typeset by Marssaié Jordan
Printed and bound in the UK

A CIP catalogue record for this book
will be available from the British Library

ISBN: 9781999642570

2 4 6 8 10 9 7 5 3 1

To the weirdos

# SUNNY

# 1

# FRIDAY

Dear Diary,

It's been a while. And because you're back, because I brought you back (after spiralling your backbone back into place)—backity back back back—Aurelia, for some reason, feels like she needs to be introduced to you all over again. Like she don't know you. Like she don't remember you. But I do. So we don't have to shake hands and do the whole "my name is" thing. But Aurelia might need to do that. Today she asked me if I still call you Diary, or if I call you Journal now. Or maybe Notebook. I told her Diary. I've always called you that. Because I like Diary. Notebook, no. And Dear Journal doesn't really work the same. Doesn't do it for me.

Dear Diary is better, not just because of the double *D* alliteration action, but also because Diary reminds me of the name Darryl, so at least I feel like I'm talking to an actual someone. And Darryl reminds me of the word "dairy," and "dairy" and "diary" are the same except for where *i* is. And I like dairy. At least milk. I can't drink a lot of it, which you know, because it makes my stomach feel like it's full of glue, which you also know. But I like it anyway. Because I'm weird. Which you definitely know. You know I like weird stuff. And everything about milk is weird. Even the word "milk," which I think probably sounds like what milk sounds like when you guzzle it. Milkmilkmilkmilkmilk. I should start over.

Dear Diary,

This is my start over.

Aurelia asked me how long it's been since I've spoken to you. I told her, a while. When I was a little kid and was all yelly-yelly and Darryl wanted me to be more hushy-hushy, he gave me you and told me to put the noise on your pages whenever I felt like I needed to, which was all the time except for when I was running or sleeping. Told me to fold it up in you, so he could get some peace. So he could have quiet for concentration when we picked at our puzzles after work. Yes, Diary, we still do puzzles together. It's still our way of, I guess, bonding. Anyway, after a while, my brain stopped pushing so much loud out of my mouth. Stopped noisey-ing up the puzzling. Thanks to you.

You know how a health bar makes you less hungry, but don't really make you full? Diary, that's what you are. A health bar. You take the hunger-growl out of my mind. And once I got to a place where the growl was pretty much a purr, I stopped writing in you.

But now the volume on the growl is turning up again. And even though it's being turned up, I can feel it working its way down, pushing behind my eyes, and marching over my tongue, ready to come out. And my father, well, he still doesn't want to be disturbed. And I don't want to disturb him and his work, and his newspaper, and definitely not the puzzles, because the puzzles are our time. So, Diary, thanks for still being a friend. Something for me to bite down on. Something for me to whisper-scream to. Because sometimes I have too many screams up there. And they boing boing in my brain

boing boing in my brain like a jumping bean,

boing boing in my brain like a jumping bean my brain a bouncy castle at a party nobody's invited to.

And now I can put them in you, again.

And now Aurelia's asking me about it. About you. Asking me about journaling. No. Diary-ing. Which sounds like diarrhea-ing. Which is sorta the same thing. Aurelia told me she thinks it's a good thing I've been writing again. Even wanted to make sure I understood that whatever I write down don't have to make sense as long as it's really me. Really my brain and heart stuff. And that's a good thing, even though I already knew that, because making sense makes no sense to me. Sense should kinda already be made, right? It should already exist like love, or maybe sky. You don't have to create it or choreograph it or nothing like that. At least I don't think you do. So none of this has to make sense, it just has to make … me, me. I'm already me, but it has to make me… something. Make me quiet and calm, and maybe also make me brave enough to do what I'm going to have to do tomorrow at the track meet, which is probably not going to be quiet or calm. That's the real reason Aurelia's interested in you, Diary. She thinks I don't know that, but I know. I know because I know she knows I'm scared. That's why I brought you back. I'm so scared. And scared don't sound like eek. Or gasp. Scared sounds like glass. Shattering.

Scared sounds like glass shattering.

Diary, after all these years, you ever not want to be written in? On? Am I writing on you or in you? Or both? And how does that make you feel? I've never really asked you that. You ever just want to stay blank? Just be paper or whatever you think you are? Because I know what that's like. And tomorrow, my father will too.

Also, Aurelia called you a journal, but you're a diary, so I will call you by your name.

# 2
# SATURDAY

Dear Diary,

I know—at least I think I know—everything has a sound connected to it. Has a tick or a boom. Or some- thing. Like a *tickboom*. Or a *tick-tickboom*. Or a *tick-bada-bada-boom-bap-bap-ooh*. Or a ... I'm weird. I'm not really weird. I'm just . . . *tickboom*. Yeah.

It's been three weeks, and something like 1,814,400 ticks since I was watching Patina

watching *Patina*,

watching *Patina*,

*tee*-nuh, *tee*-nuh,

*tick-tick boom* and come from behind and crush the last leg of her first 4x800 relay. Sounded like shum-*swip!-shum-swip!-shum-swip!-shum-swip!* all the way to the feta-feta-finish line.

She was cheesin', and the crowd . . . went . . . wild. *Cushhhhh!* Deja and Krystal and Brit-Brat went wild. *Cushhhhh!* Coach and Whit went wild. Curron and Aaron and Mikey went wild. *Cushhhhhh! Cushhhhh!* Ghost and Lu went wild. Threw their arms around me while Patty did some kind of power strut over to us, a winner. Wih- wih-*winner*. Wih-*winner*. Patty's a *winner*. A big *winner*. Number *tenner*, and a *grinner*, a bleep bloop *blinner*, that's not a word but I'm a *beginner*, not like Patty, Patty's a *winner*, wih-*winner*.

Okay, I'm weird.

Diary, you know I'm also a winner. Wih-*winner*. Which, for me, is boring. Buh-boring. And sounds like snore. Snuh-*snoring*. My race always, always, always sounds like other people talking. Like no one really caring that I'm running a mile—1600 meters—faster than they can probably run a block. Like, *chick chick chick chick chick chick chick chick chick, check me out! Chick chick chick chick chick chick chick chick, check me out!* But no one does, until the last lap. Which is the part where I win. Week after week. Wih-wih winner . . . whatever.

I give the ribbons to Darryl. Whatever.

He says something about my mother.
Whatever.

*Your mother would want you to work harder.*

*What's wrong with you?*

*She'd want you to tighten that form. Widen your stride. Beat your time.*

*Like I always say, ROI. Return on Investment.*

*What's wrong with you?*

*The more you put in, the more you get out.*

*That last lap, open up your lungs. Breathe.*

*Your mother would want you to breathe.*

*What's wrong with you?*

And then I immediately start thinking about what breathing sounds like. I can never really find it. Always just on the tip of my tongue. And then I start thinking about what not breathing sounds like. And then, while Darryl goes on and on about my mother, I start thinking about crying. Me, crying. Not me crying right then, but me crying when I was being born. And how I didn't. Not at first. That's what Darryl always tells me, has no problem telling me. That I didn't cry. Because I wasn't breathing. And my mother was crying. Then I started breathing. Then she stopped. And I started crying.

*Ships passing in the night.*

She's not here because I am. Because of me. Because something is wrong with me, Diary, which made something wrong with her. Her. She has a name. She *had* a name. Has. You remember? It's Regina. Regina Lancaster. Born on Rosa Parks's birthday, delivered me on the day of a hurricane. And died.

Dear Diary,

"Amniotic embolism."

Those words are like confetti for the tongue. Like speaking a foreign language. Hypnotic symbolism, amniotic embolism. So much fun to say, but it means "death of my mother" when you translate it into birth-giving talk. Means her blood was poisoned. Means it caused her heart to stop. Means me, as a kid, yelling all the time looking for her, searching for a beat.

Diary, I know you already know this. It's been written in me for a long time, so I know I've written it in you a long time ago. Along with questions. Questions like, do you know what it feels like to feel like a murderer? I do. At least I did back then. And I still do. Sometimes. Don't get me wrong, Darryl has never called me that or said anything like that. If anything, he says it was the amniotic embolism that did it. But he's always telling me over and over again that I owe it to my mother to accomplish her dreams of being a marathon winner. For her. Not just a runner, a winner. And he's been pushing me from the beginning. I don't really know if I mean that, like for real, but . . . I might, because it might be true. When I was learning to walk, soon as I took my first pitter-patter, Darryl probably pushed me. Like, really pushed me. That's just how he is. Not hard or nothing. Just a little bump to make those steps quicker. Laps around the house by four. On the track by five. Marathon talk by six. As if not having a mother can be wiped away by a medal. Figured I'd start by mastering the mile.

But the thing is, the mile don't have enough sound for me. Never did. There's only the *chick chick chick* my feet make on the track for 1600 meters, which after a while sounds almost like nothing. *Chick chick chick* becomes *chih chih chih* becomes *ch ch ch* underneath everybody's chatter about what they're gonna do as soon as these last few long laps are over, scrolling on their phones, *check check checking*, refreshing, then scrolling some more.

I needed something else, something other than the stupid mile. Than the stupid win. So earlier today— three boring weeks, three victorious meets after Patty's crazy comeback—I finally put some sound in my mile. Some *pooshhh*, or *skweeb*.

Diary, what does it sound like to stop? Like,

*skurrt!* I was three laps in, coming up on the fourth. *Chick chick-ing* around the track, zoning out. I'm on the first turn of the last lap, no one even close to me. I'm cruising, *ch ch ch* heading in for the win. And then.

I changed my mind.

Just pulled up, stopped running, started walking.

Sound.

The crowd goes wild! *Whaaaa?* Deja and Krystal and Brit-Brat go wild. *Whaaaa?* Ghost and Lu and Patty go wild. *Whaaaa?* Curron and Aaron and Mikey go wild. *Whaaa?* Coach and Whit go really wild. *WHAAAA?*

Then the crowd goes *whooooop!* as the other runners gallop past me, burning whatever fuel they had left, barrelling toward the finish line.

From the sideline, Coach scream-asked what I was doing, and I just smiled and clapped for the other runners. Then Coach yelled something else mad. His words sounded like crumpled paper. Up in the bleachers Darryl popped straight up in the middle of the crowd. Some people were laughing, some mad, some totally confused.

Those were the best ones. The confused ones. The faces that looked like they were made of wax, and had been melted and remodelled. Like, *skwilurp bleep blurp squish*. My father's face didn't look like that. It didn't look melted or squishy at all. My father's face had the look. A look I was used to, but hated. Like a stone becoming more of a stone. And what sound does that make? I think, for my dad, the same sound that breathing makes. A sound I can't seem to find, even though it's on the tip of my tongue.

Dear Diary,

One more thing about today. I almost bit my tongue off. Just nibbled too hard on it the whole ride home. And if I did bite it off, it would've been so gross, because then I would've had blood on my teeth. And what if my father, for some reason, cracked a joke or said something funny that made me smile and then he would've had to see my cherry chompers? My bloody reds? But he didn't. And why would he? There was nothing funny, at least not to him. He just bit down on his own tongue, and judging by the dimple in his cheek going in and out, he was biting down pretty hard too.

It was a quiet ride with nothing but the *whirr whirr* of the air conditioner, a *ssssss* that sounded more like air leaking out of something than seeping into it.

The cat had my father's tongue.

Diary, do you know where that saying came from? Cat got your tongue? Me neither. I mean, think about it. It's like, you're saying a cat jumped up and shoved its face in my mouth and bit down on my tongue? And is it a cat that looks like a tiger, with the stripes? Or maybe a black cat? Definitely a black cat. Or one of those grey cats that people call blue, even though grey and blue are different colors. But they sound the same. They both sound like a shaky violin, which sounds like a cat crying. Just before it jumps up and bites your tongue off.

Anyway, my dad was the cat, with his own face in his own mouth biting his own tongue. Making him more quiet than usual. A quiet that was thick and itchy like carpet on skin. Because I knew he had a lot to say. How could he not? I'd just lost. Not even lost, gave up. Not really gave up. Gave in. That's what I did, forfeited my race, and I knew for a fact he wanted to know why. Didn't he have some story he was dying to blab about? Something about how my mum would be disappointed?

*Regina wasn't a quitter.*

Or, *Before you, I had never seen anything, anyone, beat her.*

Or his favorite, *What's wrong with you?* Something to remind me of what I can't remember. He had to have something to say, and this was the perfect opportunity for Darryl to talk my head off, put it back on, talk it off again, then kick it down the street, then look at headless me and talk my . . . neck off.

That was way worse than the cat-got-your-tongue thing.

What I'm trying to say is, Darryl wouldn't say a word. And I knew better than to ask him if he wanted to know why I did it. Why I stopped. And why today, a week before my thirteenth birthday, her deathday. Not that he'd flip out and do something crazy, like bite his own tongue off and show me bloody teeth— even though, honestly, I would've rather seen that, than . . . *that look* again. But I would've taken that look if it meant we could've talked about it.

I guess I'll just talk to you about it until I can talk to Aurelia about it first thing Monday morning. Which means I have to get through the rest of this weekend, like a tongue trapped in a shut mouth. Like a feather somehow trapped in stone. Like a *thwip* attached to a *thump*.

# 3
# SUNDAY

Dear Diary,

Diary-ing's not for Sundays.

And it's not that I don't have nothing to say, or that I don't want to say it. I just think maybe you deserve a day off to be as blank and closed as you want.

I know I feel that way sometimes.

# 4

# MONDAY

Dear Diary,

Just so you know, Sundays at my house are still basically just Darryl in his boxers sitting in his chair— their chair—reading his boring business magazines about, I guess, ROI, and crinkling up the newspaper, no telling if he really reads the thing, but he definitely crinkles it a lot. And coffee. And cold. Because the house is too big for warm.

This giant castle. So big. Too big for just the two of us. A dining room, a kitchen, a living room, a family room—which, by the way, is where the puzzles are put together. So big there could be other people living here and we wouldn't even know it. How funny would that be? Another family living on the other side of the house.

Maybe a dad who would go to work in a suit. But not a regular suit. A tracksuit. Hmmm. What would he be doing? Maybe he'd be a gym teacher. No. Not that. A dance instructor. And maybe he wouldn't have a son. Maybe he'd have a daughter, and his daughter's name would be … Moony. And maybe Moony wouldn't have to write in diaries—not that there's anything wrong with you. And maybe Moony has a mother. And maybe that mother reads the newspaper all day, and sometimes she looks over at Moony and winks, in between taking sips of coffee, and maybe her coffee doesn't make the whole house smell like it's been sprinkled with sugar and set on fire like my father's does.

All Darryl does all day is takes a sip, then crinkles the paper. Flips the page. Takes a sip. Crinkles the paper. Flips the page. And after a whole Sunday of that—you didn't miss much—the simple *ding-dong* of the doorbell this morning basically sounded like disco to me.

Dear Diary,

The only thing weirder than me is my teacher creature. Aurelia. I know I said she might feel like she has to introduce herself to you again, even though she's been around as long as you have, but I just realized that it's been years, so maybe you don't remember her. Maybe it's you who needs the again-introduction.

Aurelia has blue hair. Sometimes. Sometimes it's purple. Sometimes orange.

Aurelia has fingernails that always look like they've been painted by tiny artists with tiny brushes.

Aurelia's clothes always look dirty, even though they always smell clean. "Clirty" is a word I've made up to describe the look.

Aurelia has tattoos all over her. Weird ones. Loopy and lopsided stars that look like I did them. With my eyes closed. She even has tattoos on her hands. On her fingers. Her knuckles. Big letters that on one hand say S-T-A-Y, and on the other, B-U-S-Y.

Remember?

If not, just know Aurelia is part of the plan. I know you don't know this part, Diary, because I didn't know this part until last year. (Know that no know is a no-no.) She was part of my parents' original plan. I don't (know!) the whole plan, or if it was actually written down in outlines and graphs and charts and diagrams and codes, or how far they even got. But from what I know, my mum and Darryl, who, by the way, were boyfriend-girlfriend since they were my age, which by the way, means they'd basically been lovey-dovey for infinity times infinity, which by the way means great grossness and gross greatness, were planning to graduate from middle school, go to high school, be king and queen of all the things (most likely to succeed at being boyfriend-girlfriend), get scholarships to university, where my mother would study psychology and my father would study business (even though he loved taking pictures), then graduate and go to more school to study the same things over again, which seems . . . I don't know, the opposite of smart.

But that's what my parents did. School, then more school.

And after more school, once they both got fancy jobs in offices with carpeted floors and phone answerers and vending machines with trail mix and fruit snacks, they would buy this giant house, then move on to step four of the plan—or is it step five?—which was to make me, and I was going to be named Sunny whether I was a boy or a girl.

The next step in the plan was to homeschool me, which just means go to school at home, and Aurelia was supposed to be my teacher, all along. According to the plan.

And so she is. And I'm glad she's here.

Crazy thing is, Diary, you weren't part of the plan.

But I'm glad you're here too.

Dear Diary,

Aurelia laughed at Darryl this morning. She was coming in and he was going out and he said good-bye to me, but it was in a weird way, like the words were coming through his throat but not actually out of his mouth, and Aurelia thought that was funny and asked him what was wrong with him. He said nothing was wrong with him, but Aurelia knew that wasn't true. Not just because of the way he was talking, but also because of the way he was looking. He wears a grey or blue suit every day, and today it was a grey one, but it was wrinkled, and one of the trouser legs was too long, so he looked like half of him had shrunk overnight.

She asked me why he looked like he had just run a mile in his business suit.

Him need to fix his hem. That's what she said in a baby voice, and it was funny until she asked me what his problem was, and I told her he hadn't really said too much to me since Saturday's race. Or . . . not-race. Aurelia knew I was going to do it, and she gave me a high five before shaking her head and saying, Him need to fix his attitude.

And his hem. Then she told me that I needed to fix us pancakes.

For breakfast.

And for maths.

This is what homeschool is like for me now, Diary. I don't remember if I told you what it was like for me back then, but that's probably because homeschool back then just felt like ... day. Like nothing to talk about. Like nothing different. But now I know it's different because everyone on my team has to go to school—outside school inside of a building—and they complain about bullies—at least Ghost does—and Patty's always going on about hair flippers, whoever they are. So I know my version of school isn't like theirs at all.

First pancakes. Turn a recipe for six into a recipe for two. If I do it right, I eat the pancakes. If I do it wrong, I have to watch Aurelia eat all the pancakes (extra syrup) and I have to eat a health bar (extra health).

Then science class. Which today was dissecting a health bar. Because I had pancakes for breakfast. Because division comes pretty natural to me.

Thankfully. So, yeah. Turns out a health bar has a lot of funny-sounding stuff in it that actually seems kind of weird. Also, they taste like dirt. I know, because I've had dirt.

After that, English. Right now I'm learning Shakespeare. You know Shakespeare? Wait, first let's talk about that name—Shakespeare. Shake a spear in your face. Tell you to back up off me before I . . . do something bad. Like . . . recite you some poetry that sounds like,

Thee thither thather rather in rhythm,
Dost thou knowest such promise of prism, O
hallowed light! All swallowed by night! O
am nee ah tick em buh lism!

Seriously, Diary. His name is like a warning. And for good reason. His work is hard. But Aurelia makes it fun. She acts out the plays and stuff. *Romeo and Juliet*. I love you, no, I love you. We have to be together. But we can't. But we have to. Oh, but we can't so now we have to die. Made me think of my parents, but only until Aurelia turned on this movie called *West Side Story*, which she said is just like Shakespeare's *Romeo and Juliet*, except with gangs and knives and snapping and dancing. That makes me think I might want to join a gang. Of dancers.

And then social studies. We do a lot of different things, but today we went to the museum. One of my favourite things to do. We wandered the big halls, staring up at the walls, reading about war and art, gazing at soldiers who wore white ponytail wigs, and queens and kings wrapped in bandages and buried in gold, and castles and constitutions and letters like these, and on and on. Until we finally sat down and just looked at other people looking at the things we just looked at. Watched their heads swivel as they read, and their fingers point, sometimes too close to the art. Watched old people hold hands and creep around. Old people whose brains are probably just as museum-y as the museum. Romeos and Juliets, who I bet had pancakes for breakfast, and health bars in their back pockets.

Dear Diary,

There's so much I need to tell you about now, but there's also a lot I need to tell you about then. You missed a lot when I put you away. You missed a lot since I stopped making noise. Since I stopped asking about her. Since I stopped screaming about how bad I miss her, how I don't know what it means to miss her but know that I feel like one trouser leg is always too long. Like something just don't fit. Since I got okay at keeping my mother inside, so that I didn't upset Darryl.

One of the things you missed is really important, but before I tell you, I have to tell you about the time Aurelia took me to get a tattoo. It was a few years ago. We were at the museum, having our usual social studies class, this time staring at old sculptures. I remember there was this one that we were looking at. A statue of a lady as white as Lu. She looked like she might've been about to do some kind of dance move, maybe a spin, but couldn't quite whip it right because the artist forgot to make arms for her. And all of a sudden, while looking at the armless lady, Aurelia just started crying. I told her it was okay that the lady didn't have arms because it was just a statue. And Aurelia said that wasn't why she was crying. That she was crying because it was her anniversary. And then I told her that I didn't know she was married. And she said she wasn't, which really confused me, and my confused became confused-er when she all of a sudden was like, *Let's go get a tattoo.*

I was thinking what you're thinking right now, Diary. I was thinking WHAT? But she didn't mean we were getting tattoos. She meant *she* was going to get a tattoo, and I was going to come with her. Art class.

Have you ever been to a tattoo place? Actually, I know the answer to that one. You haven't. But I have. There was art all over the walls, and books and books of sketches of googly-eyed dragons and hearts with knives stabbed in them and dripping fruit and all kinds of other stuff. And a lady who looked like she liked the same things Aurelia liked sat behind the counter in the front of the place. She was bald and had a tattoo of a corner store on the side of her head.

I remember her. I'll never forget her. And I'll never forget Fish.

Fish was this big, big, big dude—the guy who tattooed Aurelia. He was like a walking wall. And if he was really a wall, he would've been like a wall in my house. Clean. Plain. No marks. No colour. No art nowhere. Seems weird for a house. Seemed weirder for a tattooer.

And I'll never forget him asking Aurelia how many years she's celebrating, but he said it like *How many is it, again?* like he was supposed to know. And Aurelia saying this was her twentieth anniversary. And him asking if she wanted another star, and her saying yes but in a different colour. And him asking what colour, and Aurelia turning to me and asking me what colour, and me saying green. But not just any green. *Go* green. And I'll never forget him pulling out this weird little machine that buzzed like it had a tiny lawnmower engine inside of it, if there was a such thing as tiny lawnmowers, and dipping it in what looked like green paint, then scratching another ugly star into Aurelia's wrist. And while he was doing it, dragging that buzzing machine over her skin a few times, scraping green into brown, Aurelia told me a story to keep her mind off the pain.

The story was about how she got hooked on drugs when she was in college. Yeah, I was surprised too! Aurelia said her boyfriend introduced them to her and she just got ... lost. She said the only people there to help her were my parents. They pretty much dragged her to get help. Especially my mother, who, after Aurelia got out of drug rehab, begged her to come to a dance class with her so she could stay busy and keep her mind off getting lost again. And this dance class was going to help Aurelia stay found. That's when I found out my mother used to dance. According to Aurelia, my mother wasn't very good at it, but still.

After Aurelia's first year clean, she and my mother got really, really bad star tattoos as a way to celebrate. And Aurelia kept doing it every year after. Tattoo after tattoo. Star after star. Kept dancing, too. And my mother made Darryl promise to keep Aurelia close— keep an eye on her—keep her busy, which is how she ended up my teacher. Part of the plan.

Oh, and I'll never forget asking Fish why they called him Fish, since he didn't look like . . . a fish. And instead of just answering, he lifted his shirt up over his head, and there was a picture of Aurelia tattooed on his big belly.

Aurelia Simone Fisher.

Fish was the boyfriend. The one she was messed up with when they were younger. The amateur tattoo artist who gave her the first star in her galaxy.

That was the day I decided to never do drugs. And the day I decided that when I got old enough, I would get a tattoo that covered my whole stomach. It's going to be of three ships, but not on water. On land. And, most importantly— the thing you missed—that was the day Aurelia started teaching me to dance.

Dear Diary,

Yes. I dance.

I know. A lot has changed.

I guess you could say, dancing with Aurelia is like P.E. class. We kick our shoes off, then move whatever we can move out of the way in the living room of my house to make enough space—a pretend dance floor with carpet the same ashy colour as cardboard, but not as easy to break-dance on. We move the coffee table, and some of the smaller things, but the chair, my father's chair—*their* chair—we leave alone. Darryl's told me a bunch of times that he and my mother bought the chair as their first piece of furniture together. He had just landed his big-time business job doing whatever he does with numbers and money and ROI, and was going to help my mother open up her own therapy office. Her own space to talk to people about their lives, and what they're scared of, and how dreaming sounds to them, and the first thing she and my father bought together— for her—was the thing to make the clients more comfortable. This chair. It's soft purple, and leans back, and Darryl's always lint-rolling it, and brushing its bulky arms softly with the palms of his hands, like patting a son that's made him proud.

So me and Aurelia don't mess with it. Just leave it alone and pretend it's our only audience member. Aurelia calls it Harry Chairy. I call it Chair. Like Cher. You know who that is, Diary? Well, if you don't, just know she makes pretty good dance music.

And Aurelia makes pretty good dance moves. Out of anything. She can make them out of ballet. I know you know what ballet is, but just in case you don't, it's tip-top, tiptoe, total body control. Sounds like ocean. Like rolling waves. She also does tap, but never brings her shoes with her because you can't hear the tappity-tapping on carpet either. She does modern dance, which is like . . . I don't know. It doesn't really feel all that modern. Not to me. But I guess it's more like theater dance. Like drama. Kind of stuff they do in the *West Side Story* movie. Snap, snap. And, my favorite, hip-hop. Now this is what I'm talking about. This is what I've *been* talking about, what

I meant when I said every move has a sound. A tick or a boom, or something. Like a tickboom. Or a *tick-tickboom*. Or, in this case:

*Hit and hit and ugh and ooooh, clap and aye, and owwww, whoosh*
*Hit and hit and ugh and ooooh, clap and aye, and owwww, whoosh*

to go with these moves:

*Shrug and shrug and kick and slide back, clap and dab and body roll, spin*
*Shrug and shrug and kick and slide back, clap and dab and body roll, spin*

And Aurelia always tells me to end . . . with *attitude*. Which basically always seems to be me ending with a big cheese on my face. So instead of ending like *what!* I always end like *wow!* But Aurelia don't mind.

Dear Diary,

Aurelia knew that I was going to have to confront Coach at practice about what happened Saturday at the meet, so she asked me if I was nervous when we pulled up to the park. I had basically been quiet after the dancing, and on the whole ride to practice. I told her I was nervous, a little. But really, I was nervous . . . *a lot*. And then she asked me if I was sure I wanted to even be there. Like, if Darryl wasn't so hard on me about running, would I still want to be on the team at all? Diary, she was talking to me about how I did what I said I was going to do, and when I was going to do it, so that I didn't feel like I was disrespecting my mum by quitting on the day she died or on the day she gave birth to me, and I could hear everything Aurelia was saying—it wasn't going all womp womp or nothing like that— but at the same time I was staring out at the track. Watched for a second as Lu and Ghost slapped hands. Patty and Aaron laughed at something. Brit-Brat and Deja were talking to Whit. And Coach was sitting on the bench on the side with his phone to his ear. And... I don't know. Something about seeing everybody just made me feel like I belonged. I know that's a little cheesy. But it's true. So I told Aurelia that I would. That I wanted to be there, on this team, with these people. And then I got out of the car. And suddenly I didn't feel so good. From cheesy to queasy... easy.

The walk from the car to the track was a long one. And all I could think about was, what was my plan? In my mind there was an outline:

I. OPTION 1: APPROACH COACH (and avoid rhyming)

A. Sit down next to him and tie your shoes and say "Fancy seeing you here."

B. Approach him like *West Side Story,* *snap, snap, snap, snap.*

C. Walk straight up to him and slap him in the face so he'll be forced to talk about something else.

## II. OPTION 2: DON'T APPROACH COACH

    A. Run directly onto the track.

    B. Turn around and walk back to the car before Aurelia leaves.

    C. Finally try to activate my teleportation powers.

And a chart:

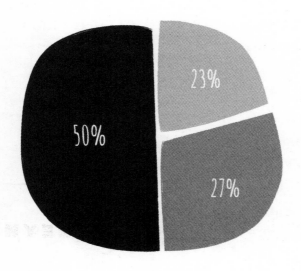

- TELL COACH HOW YOU FEEL
- GO HOME AND MAKE MORE PANCAKES
- DON'T TELL COACH HOW YOU FEEL

50%

23%

27%

And also a graph:

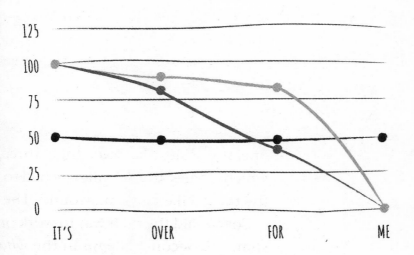

● ME, IF I TALK TO COACH
● BOOMTICK (SILVER LINING)
● ME, IF I DON'T TALK TO COACH

Figured it was better to be safe than sorry. But still didn't think to pack a sick bag, and the pancakes I had this morning had turned back into batter. A bitter batter, pitter-pattering up my throat.

Dear Diary,

Don't worry. I didn't puke. But I wanted to when Coach called my name and waved me over,  and then yelled it louder and told me to hustle up, and that's when I wanted to puke myself out of myself, like *blooepp* and just lay there on the ground, a slimy brown ooze.

Aaron was leading the stretches in that way-too-serious way he does, and Lu was mimicking him in that way-too-silly way he does, and Ghost and Patty were trying not to laugh, and Coach barked at them and told them he had enough going on and not to make it a long week. And I wished I was with them trying not to laugh, but I was too busy trying to imagine ways to pull the cat out of my mouth.

I was also wondering if maybe I was Coach's *enough going on.*

Next thing I knew, Coach was standing in front of me, telling me to pick my head up and look at him, and asking me what happened on Saturday. He said at first he thought I caught a cramp or something, but then said he saw me smiling and knew it couldn't have been a cramp, unless it was a cramp in the mind. I told him I didn't know how to explain it.

He said, Try.

I said, I don't know how to say it.

He said, Try harder.

And I just stood there as all the thoughts went boing boing in my brain. Thoughts about how maybe I could just lie. But I'm not a liar. But I could just tell him I stopped running because I wanted to give everybody else from other teams a chance to feel what it feels like to win—a half lie has to be better than a whole lie, right?—and that it would even add some extra spice to it for the crowd, and then the next week I would be back to winning, except I didn't want to actually run anymore, so even just the thought of saying that made me feel jumpy. But still, I didn't want to say . . . *everything*.

Coach said he was waiting. He cocked his head. Folded his arms.

I looked down.

*Up, up!*

I looked up. And told him I stopped running because . . . I was tired.

He asked me what I meant by that. Said it didn't sound right.

I told him, It was right, though. I was tired. I am tired.

Coach cocked his head to the other side, and I could tell he was getting fizzy inside.

So was I. Like a bottle of fizzy drink with bubbles rising up through the body, up the neck. And then, suddenly, *blooepp*. Just . . . came out. All the sound that sounded like *I don't want to run no more, Coach*. That sounded like *because, like I already told you, my mother died giving birth to me, and my father is mad at me, and that's the only reason I run, but I didn't do nothing. I didn't do nothing. I don't want to do this no more.*

Diary, here's the thing. You can't really be on a track team if you don't want to run. I know that. But I didn't want to run. And I still wanted to be on the team. Because I'm weird. So Coach, who was now less fizzy, asked me what I wanted to do. I told him I didn't know. Then he told me I couldn't be on the team no more, that it just didn't make sense to keep me if I wasn't running.

I wanted to tell him it doesn't have to make sense, but then he said he still loved me and wanted to see if he could help me with whatever else I wanted to do. And I asked him if he was serious, and he said he was.

I said, Anything?

He said, anything, but I just needed to tell him what that was. So.

I told him I wanted to dance. He said, Dance?

I said, Dance. And then I hit my routine. Just *blooepp'd* it right out of me.

Dear Diary,

I have to admit it wasn't my best exhibition of my dancing ability. My booms and ticks were a little off, probably because I was just so . . . I don't know. This was Shakespeare-level stressful. Plus, it was still kind of a new routine Aurelia was teaching me. I hadn't really mastered it yet.

Coach didn't know what to say, so he didn't say nothing. For a while. Maybe ten seconds. Felt like ten minutes. Ten hours. I could hear Curron from the track saying something, and I couldn't make out what it was, but I knew it was about me because I heard Patty shut it down. Then I heard Whit shut Patty's shutdown down. Coach glanced over to the track just for a moment, then turned back to me, his expression still stuck as if he was wearing a plastic Halloween mask of his own face. Honestly, I thought he was going to laugh, so I looked down, that way I wouldn't see it. But then he told me to look up. As usual.

Wow.

That's what he said, Diary. Wow.

And then he told me that unfortunately he doesn't know any dance squads, dance groups, dance teams, dance troupes, or dance clubs. Not sure why he had to say it all those different ways, but I could tell he didn't mean it in a mean way. Still kind of stung, though. But then the strangest thing happened. I mean, I still can't believe it, even right now as I'm writing this to you. In you. Coach stared at me for few more hour-minute seconds, mumbling something under his breath. Mumbling, mumbling, mumbling. By the way, I just realized something—*mumble* is the sound of mumbling. Kind of like milk. And I had that milk feeling in my stomach still when all of a sudden Coach told me to do the *whoosh* part again. And that's how he said it.

He said, *Sunny, do the* whoosh *part.* The *whoosh* part. The spin. That's what he was talking about.

*Whoosh* is the sound of spinning.

I was confused, but I did it. I followed directions because Coach is . . . Coach.

I *whooshed.* He told me to do it one more time. So I *whooshed* again. And then he told me to follow him.

Diary, I was so, so, soooo confused. One second I'm one second away from guts on the ground, the next second I'm boomticking in front of Coach, and the next next second I'm standing at the back of his car, watching him dig around in the boot. And you know what he asked me, Diary, after tossing duffel bags and jerseys and other kinds of things to the left and to the right? You know what he said after he slowly stepped back, holding the thing he'd been looking for?

*Do you know what a discus is?* That's what he said. I just said yes.

And then Coach asked me if I wanted to try throw- ing it. For the team.

And I asked him why I would ever do that. I'm a runner. At least I was.

And Coach spun around and said, *Whoosh.* Then he spun again, looking like an amateur dancer, but like a proper discus thrower, and said, *Whoosh.*

And . . . I understood. It was dancing. Discus was dancing. Discus was . . . disco.

I said yes.

I mean, I said I'll try.

Dear Diary,

There's a song by that lady, Cher, I was telling you about. The lady I named the chair, Chair, after. Yeah. It goes, *Do you believe in life after love?*

But it sounds like, *Do you bee-LEEEEEEEVE in life after love?*

*after love?* <——echo

*after love?* <——echo

Dear Diary,

Patty, Lu, and Ghost caught me talking to the discus. I was sitting on the bench, waiting for practice to be over, and was imagining the metal disk as a spaceship with tiny aliens inside and my job was to figure out how to throw it back into space or something. To Planet Discobulus, maybe. A planet made of sparkles and glass and beats that make the aliens pump their fists and wave their arms around like snakes. And maybe that's how they communicate. Or maybe their language is just bass. Like, *oont, oont, oont, oont, oont*. And right when I was *oonting*, Lu and Ghost and Patty walked up.

Ghost asked me if I was talking to the thing.

Patty told him the thing was called a discus.

Ghost asked if I was talking to the discus.

I told him I was. Because . . . I was.

Lu asked what I was doing with it.

Patty asked why Lu and Ghost were asking stupid questions.

Then she asked a smart one. Really, the only one.

Why did I quit running Saturday?

I told her, and them, I was tired of it, and actually quit running today. Quit the team.

And the crowd goes wild. In a bad way. Until I told them I danced for Coach.

And the crowd goes silent. In a weird way. Then the crowd goes laughing. In a laughing way. Then Coach comes over. And the crowd goes home.

But only after Coach told them that I am—will be—the Defenders' first discus thrower. *Cushhhhhh.*

Dear Diary,

Guess what? The cat finally let go of Darryl's tongue. And when it did, I happened to be sitting in the car next to him with a discus in my lap. Maybe it was the discus that scared the cat away.

*What's that?* Which is all he said.

What's this?

I told him it was a discus, that I would be throwing it. Then he asked how I could practice running the mile and throwing the discus. And then I told him I quit running the mile. And me saying that was like taking a heavy cat, a lion, off my back—digging the claws out—and shoving it along with the other cat right back in Darryl's mouth.

When we got home, I ran upstairs to change my clothes and to kiss my discus. Not sure why, but I kind of just feel like it needs to know I love it if it's going to work with me. If we're going to do this thing together. I know . . . weird. But it wasn't like, smoochy smoochy muah muah smoochy smooch smoochington, or nothing like that. Just a regular one.

When I got back downstairs, Darryl was sitting in his chair in the living room with a needle and thread, fixing up the hem of his jacked-up pants. While I poured myself a glass of water (honestly, I just wanted to wash my lips off), Darryl laid his pants across the chair and went into the family room, where he stood over the big table, puzzle pieces scattered all over.

This is the way it goes almost every night, unless Mr. Nico comes by. Mr. Nico is the reason for all the puzzles in the first place. I didn't know this when I was younger, but when Darryl made his first business transaction thingy, it was with Mr. Nico. He invested in Mr. Nico's company, which is a puzzle company. It's called Puzzle Peace. You take a picture, e-mail it in, and they send you a puzzle of the picture. Simple. Only catch is there is no map or key. The boxes come with nothing on them. You don't know what you're going to see until you see it. So when I was growing up, me and Darryl would work on puzzles of my mother every single day. Darryl had taken so many pictures of her, and them, almost like he wanted us to have enough images to piece together for the rest of our lives.

Constant surprises. Nonstop discoveries. He used to always tell me that he wanted to make sure I knew her. At least, her face. Her smile. And I did. I do. I have to figure out how to make her—how to put it together—all the time. How to start with the edges, the borders, and work in, using my imagination. That's what Darryl taught me. And whenever we finish one, Mr. Nico brings another. Especially since free puzzles are the only "Return on Investment" my father ever gets.

Mr. Nico also smokes cigars with Darryl whenever he's here, and always asks my father if he wants to date his sister. Her name is Ms. Linda. One time Nico even slipped us a puzzle of Ms. Linda's face. That one was really a surprise. I thought she looked pretty, but we never finished it.

But Mr. Nico didn't come tonight. So Darryl didn't have to do that funny-sounding laugh he always does whenever he's asked if he'd date Ms. Linda. Instead he stood over the table, studying the pieces of a new puzzle, moving them around, looking for the corners and edges. I joined him.

And asked him if he was mad at me.
He said mad's not the word. Then I asked
what the word was.
He said he bought TV dinners.
So the word was not now.

Dear Diary,

The word is "gross."

The word is "dry."

My TV dinner tasted like an advert break.

And not a funny one, but one of the ones about life insurance. I have no idea what life insurance is, but apparently old people need it, because that's who's always on those adverts. And that's what my food tasted like.

A life insurance advert.

Or eating a puzzle.

Dear Diary,

Do you remember my room? I just realised that you've been in here the whole time, but you've been stuck in a drawer with old toys piled up on top of you. Do you remember what the walls look like? That soft green, like the colour of grass just before it gets hard in the heat? And the ceiling, flat and white? An occasional circle—a home for a lightbulb that adds more white to the white. Do you remember the carpet that looks like yarn and like yawn? Or the big plush zebra in the corner? Do you remember the baby crib? It's still there.

Dear Diary,

You're gonna throw the discus, Sunny. Sun D Runny. How you feel?

I feel great. I think. I mean, throw a little discus to the other side of the world. Know what I'm saying? Know what I'm talking about, walking about, Sunny?

Yeah, I got you. You scared Darryl gonna be mad about it?

He always mad.

True, true. He be so mad I wonder if maybe it just feels like happy to him.

Probably, but it don't feel like happy to me. Happy to me feels like *tweep tweep, beedy bip bip booyow*. That's happy. Not this *blah blah* he's doing. Not this *urrrrrrrgh, derrrrrrr, burrrr* crap. That's mad. And maybe sad.

Was that scatting? Did you just scat? Do you wanna do jazz? You could probably be a jazz singer. You got the right name.

I think that was jazz. But I'm not sure. Just sound. But if sound is jazz, then yeah. I'm Sunny the Jazz Man.

Relax, Sunny the Jazz Man, be Sunny the Discus Man first.

Or the Disco Man. No.

The Discus Man.

Okay, but after that, I'm scatting on the world, like a *scoobidee doo day deeeee*.

Yikes.

Whatever. You think maybe they got jazz dancers? You the one who should know!

I know, and I do know. They do have a kind of dance called jazz. But it don't really remind me of *flippity flap flam zingalee zay weee*. But I bet I could make a new kind of jazz dancing that goes better with scat.

Sounds like a plan. Then you'll still be *tickboom*, except now you'll be *tickboom* scat, which if you ever wanted to change your name, would be a good one to consider.

Tickboom Scat? But why would I want to change my name?

Because your father don't seem like the type to have a kid named Sunny.

But maybe my mother was. Aurelia said she was fun. She was even a dancer. But not a good one.

Just like you.

No, just like YOU. I'm a good dancer. Even excellent, sometimes.

Of course. What was I thinking? You are none other than Alvin and the Chipmunks Ailey.

I don't get it.

You wouldn't.

Whatever. She also said Darryl could dance too.

Ha! That's hard to believe. Maybe he was the real inventor of the Running Man.

I don't get that one either.

Forget it.

Forgotten.

Rotten.

Cotton.

Patty.

Patty?

Patty.

Okay.

Dear Diary,

Sorry about that last one. But talking to you is talking to you, and sometimes I need to talk to me. I don't know if that makes sense, but you know how I feel about making sense.

Goodnight.

# 5

# TUESDAY

Dear Diary,

It's Tuesday, and Tuesday is my favorite day until Thursday, because Tuesday is when me and Aurelia go to the hospital and Thursday is when we go again. I know what you're thinking. Hospitals are places people don't like to go, which is exactly the reason I love them. My grandfather works there, and we have a thing we do to bring some happy to the people who don't want to be there, but have to be.

Aurelia always brings me breakfast on these days—sausage sandwiches. So we skip the pancakes with all the cooking and measuring, and jump to the eating—by the way, sausage sandwiches are always a quadrillion times better than TV dinners, that's for sure.

At the hospital we never have to sign in. Ever. It's like we're VIP people or something. VIP. Not VIP people. That would be Very Important People people. And even though I consider myself kind of a people person, I'm not a very important person person. Just a VIP. Actually not even a VIP. Just a kid who doesn't have to sign in at the hospital because everybody, especially Ms. Melinda, who sits at the front desk, knows I'm Dr. Lancaster's grandson.

Me and Aurelia sat down in the waiting area. There are always other people waiting, some possibly even waiting for their grandfathers too, but for different reasons. Many people's faces look like water. Like if you poked their cheeks, their skin would ripple forever. A lot of times they sit in the chairs in an uncomfortable way. In a way that makes me feel like they feel like they don't have arms. Like they can't quite turn. Can't adjust. Can't feel normal until that grand- father they're waiting for comes walking through the double doors.

Then my grandfather came walking through the double doors. More like he came strutting out. He always struts. The old dude walks like walking was made just for him. Like, *ooh, yeah, ooh, yeah, you see me, walking walking wallllking.* He walks like he's holding back from dancing.

Diary, do you remember Gramps? You remember him, right? Well, he's still as good as he was the last time you heard about him. He's still helping people, still bouncing back and forth from the waiting room, to his patients' rooms, to his office, which is kind of like a tattoo shop. The only difference is the tattoo shop had posters of the outside of people's bodies, and my grandfather's office had posters of the insides of people's bodies.

His office is where he always takes us first. Which is where I told him Darryl was mad.

Gramps asked why.

And I told him because I quit running. And then Aurelia shouted, FREEDOM!

Gramps ignored Aurelia, asked me why I quit, since I've been running my whole life.

I told him, I've only been running because of my mother. Because of my father. Because of my mother.

He said because my mother was a runner.

Duh. (I didn't say that, but I thought it.)

What I said was: And she was also a dancer. So,
I'd rather move.

He looked at Aurelia.

She looked away.

Gramps said running is moving.

I said, no, dancing is.

Gramps's face turned into a question mark.

And mine, into a full stop.

Dear Diary,

Me and Aurelia don't come to the hospital to visit Gramps. I mean, we do, but we don't. We come to visit other people's Grampses. And other people's Aurelias. And sometimes, even other people's Sunnys. We go to visit patients. Not to bring them cards or flowers or gifts. We bring them something much better. The *boomity boom* and the *tickity tick*. I'm talking the *boom tick, tickboom*! But first we have to walk through all the beep beep beeps it takes to get to the cancer ward. Diary, how could a word that rhymes with "dancer" be so bad? Not to mention "answer," "prancer," and "romancer"?

Speaking of romancers: Mr. MacAfee. He has no hair. Nowhere. He's recovering after having another tumour cut out of him. Another night under the knife, another day on the drip. That's what he said when Gramps asked him how he was. But he loves Aurelia.

Always teases her by saying her name felt funny in his mouth. I laughed at that because that's what I love most about it too! Ah-RAIL-yuh.

Ms. Jenkins. We never met her before. She's new to the ward. Breast cancer. She's young, and when we came in, she was still adjusting her wig. We told her it looked good, because it did. She didn't believe us. She was also looking at a life insurance advert. I told her she didn't need that. That's only for old people.

J.J., whose real name is Jennifer—I used to call her Mrs. Jennifer, but she doesn't like to be called Mrs. anything, and even though she's too old for me to call her by her first name, she used to insist I call her just Jennifer, so I used to call her Just Jennifer, which eventually became J.J.—has lung cancer. She  wears the reddest lipstick I've ever seen.

Ian, who is my age and reads manga comics all day, has a brain tumour, Gorgeous John (his real name) has cancer in his pancreas, Ms. Felicia has stomach cancer and only watches the news, and always gets mad when we come in, and says the world's in too much danger for dancing. But we dance anyway, and anyway, she likes it.

Me and Aurelia dance for each of them.

Five, six, seven, eight . . .

*Shrug and shrug and kick and slide back, clap
and dab and body roll, spin*
*Shrug and shrug and kick and slide back, clap and
dab and body roll, spin*

And they all laugh and bop and clap and smile.
Today Ms. Jenkins even snatched her wig off and
swung it around in the air like a hair flag.

Dear Diary,

Mr. Rufus deserves his own entry.

He's much older than me, but cool. I don't know what kind of cancer Mr. Rufus has, but I know he's had it for a long time. But he's still always fun to visit. Always so happy, even though his voice is weak. Like when someone wakes you up too early on your birthday and your voice isn't all the way turned on yet, but you're still excited. That's how Mr. Rufus sounds. Whenever I see him, I do my weirdo wave, and he does a weirdo wave, which is basically just a wave, because, Diary, I don't know if you know this or not— don't know why you would—but waving is always weird. It always comes across as *yikes*.

Anyway, Mr. Rufus has bright eyes with saggy bags under them, and the brightest teeth I've ever seen. Like tiny TV screens lined up side by side. He always brags about how they're all still his, but judging by the way the nurses roll their eyes every time he says it, I think he might be lying. But that's not the reason he deserves his own page in you.

He deserves his own page because he is by far the best bed dancer I've ever seen. I mean, he really knows what he's doing. He always tells me about how he used to be a dancer on a TV show back in the day called *Soul Train*. I believe him when he says *this*. You ever heard of that show, Diary? I've never seen it, but Mr. Rufus and Aurelia and Gramps all say it was some kind of dance show. That bands would perform and young people would be dressed up on national TV showing off their booms and ticks. I asked Mr. Rufus if Cher ever came on there to perform some of her music. He just laughed at that. Not sure why. She makes great dance music.

But what I do know is that Mr. Rufus can tick with the best of them. I've seen him do it. Turn his body into real life stop-motion animation. And even though he was good at ticking, he said spinning and sliding were his specialties back in the day, and that the crowd always went crazy when he did a split. Diary, I tried to do a split once. It didn't go good. Or feel good. Anyway, when me and Aurelia and Gramps get to Mr. Rufus's room, he always adjusts the bed just enough so that he's not lying flat, and when the music comes on, he starts bopping around and jamming in the bed, as if he's trying to break loose, break free. And maybe he is. It's like he understands what dancing is for. It's not just to watch, it's to do, to somehow remind yourself that you're still . . . you. That whoever the invisible you is, the you that only talks to you, it's still alive and can add, in Mr. Rufus's words, *love, peace, and soullllllll* to the world.

Dear Diary,

Have you ever heard of Salisbury steak? It's like a hamburger drenched in a special sauce, which I guess is called Salisbury sauce. They serve it in the canteen at the hospital. Aurelia told me a while ago that Salisbury is a place, and let me tell you, the first chance I get, I'm going there. There's probably this sauce just raining down from the sky. Actually, that would be pretty messy. But maybe it's like lakes full of it. That would be better. And if that's true, I might try a new sport.

Swimming.

Dear Diary,

It's Technique Tuesday, and usually at practice I would be working on my stride, but now I don't really have a stride to work on. So it was weird. I did the usual stretches, and while I was touching my toes, and Aaron was counting out the numbers, and while Coach and Whit were off to the side looking at the clipboard, probably putting a line through my name, Lynn, who also runs the mile, asked me why I was even stretching, since I'm not a runner no more. But the way she said it, it was like she gave each word teeth.

I told her I'm still a runner, I just don't run.

She said that don't make sense.

I wanted to tell her sense don't have to be made.

It already exists.

She would've said that's stupid.

She also said I was the best in the whole league and that I'm stupid to quit.

So I got the stupid anyway.

And that's when Patty jumped in, and before she could shoot her own teeth-words at Lynn, Lu

74

jumped in to calm Patty down. Then he made a speech to everybody about how sometimes things change  in life. And how I've made a change. And how I'm still on the team and should be supported. I appreciated that.

But then Brit-Brat called him Dr. Phil. It was a joke. I kind of appreciated that, too.

And then Aaron challenged Lu. Told him he should run my race since he's so supportive. He said "supportive" in a not-very-supportive way.

Then Coach came out of nowhere and yelled at everyone, shutting it down. And all I could think about was how there is no way—zero way—Lu can run a mile. NO WAY.

NOOOOOOoOoOoo OOOOOoo WAY!

But . . . I think he'd try.

Dear Diary,

All this time I had no idea there was a concrete circle on the field. Let me explain. The track goes around a field. And in the field, down by the first two-hundred curve, there's a concrete circle. Like a bald spot. Never noticed it before. I guess the grass has always been just tall enough to disguise it.

Coach said that bald spot would be my new home. He said all my greatness is going to come out of that small space, and that what I do in that circle will affect how far I go outside of it. Or something like that. You know Coach. Actually, Diary, you don't know Coach, but if you did, you'd know that sometimes he be speaking in Shakespeare.

Since it's Technique Tuesday, and because I don't know nothing about throwing the discus, Coach wanted to just walk me through the steps. He kept telling me it was just like dancing, and to remember the *whoosh* part of my dance. The spin. Except it was going to be a double spin. A *whoosh whoosh*.

Actually, a *whoosh whoosh*, then a release. That's what Coach said.

So, a *whoosh whoosh aah*, I corrected him.

He just nodded. Took my word for it, then showed me the steps.

1. Stand straight, bend knees just a little.
2. Spread arms like wings.
3. Wind body back and forth with hands straight and stiff, cutting the air.
4. Count to three.
5. On three, spin right leg 230 degrees around. (Coach said, not 360, but not 180. I told him, 230.)

That's the first *whoosh*. I repeated those steps, again and again
        and again and
            again again again again
until practice was over. Coach said the second whoosh was coming tomorrow. I asked him, when do I actually get to throw the discus? He said first I gotta learn how to whoosh whoosh, and then my wish will be granted. *Aah.*

Dear Diary,

Darryl asked me how practice was, which was a good sign that the mad was maybe unmadding, and I told him about the discus and the whooshing and the *whoosh whooshing* and how Lu stood up for me and how Aaron told him to run a mile and how there's no way he could ever run a mile because he's never run for longer than ten seconds at a time and to run a mile like me you have to be okay with running for forever. And then Darryl cracked a little smile. Not enough to be a real smile, but still a crack in the stone.

When we got home, I made a TV dinner. When I say made, I mean microwaved. It was chicken, mashed potatoes, and peas. It all tasted like chicken, mashed potatoes, and peas, if chicken, mashed potatoes, and peas were made of plastic, and were melted. Darryl made one for himself, and while we were eating, Darryl said Gramps called him.

What he say? That's what I said.

Darryl said Gramps said he should talk to me about why I quit.

And as I tried to find my words, the doorbell rang. I can't figure out if the doorbell loves me or hates me. If that was an interruption, or some kind of bailout.

It was Mr. Nico at the door.

He came in like he usually comes in, singing, *Do you believe in life after love?* by the lady, Cher. Mr. Nico is the reason I even know who she is, because he's always singing that song, and whenever he does, it's in a jokey-joke way as a sign to let my father know that he's going to ask him about dating his sister, Ms. Linda. And that meant that Mr. Nico and my father were going to step outside and smoke cigars and talk in private, and I hate the way cigars smell, and I hate the way my father and Mr. Nico talk, so I went into the family room to work on the puzzle by myself.

So far we only had the border complete, and the top of my mother's head and forehead. And I was trying to find her eyes. But, Diary, you would be surprised how many puzzle pieces look like eyes. Or parts of eyes. Eyelashes. Eyeballs. But I got the whole left one done, and most of the right, then went upstairs to my room to try and close both of mine.

Dear Diary,

It's late and I can't sleep. Because the quiet has been unquieted. Sound. Coming through my bedroom door. I wish it was something cool, like harps or drums, or even the weird creaking of this big house "settling" as Darryl sometimes says. But, no. It's just my father choking on his own snore. Choking on his own sleep. He probably needs to adjust, roll over, or something.

He's not choking.

No, I don't think he's choking at all, actually. I think he might be crying.

# 6

# WEDNESDAY

Dear Diary,

It's Wednesday morning, and I'm pretending I didn't hear Darryl crying last night. I said good morning, and he said good morning back, which made the morning goodish. Better than the last three. But I wonder if he was just saying good morning in the same way people say fine when you ask them how they're doing, just because that's the answer everybody gives, and it's easier than the truth, which might be something like... constipated. I'm not even sure you can really have a good morning after having a bad night, and it sounded like Darryl had a bad night. And I didn't have the heart to ask about it. Don't get me wrong, I'm not freaked out from hearing him cry. Crying is crying like laughing is laughing like sense don't never have to be made because it just is. Whoa. I felt like Coach with that one. Sunny Shakespeare. Anyway, what I'm trying to say is hearing my father cry is normal.

Every time we finish a puzzle and have to take it apart, he cries.

Every birthday, he cries. His or hers. Or mine.

Every anniversary, he cries. Of their marriage. Of her death. Which is my birthday.

Every first-place ribbon, he cries. Not around me.

But at night.

But he didn't do that this weekend. There was no crying because there was no ribbon. And I learned a long time ago to never check on him. To leave him alone. When I was little, maybe like six, I asked him if he was okay and he yelled at me. And that yell was a yell like nothing I'd ever heard. It was as if my father's throat had become a revved motor, as if his eyes had become headlights, as if he had become something that would run me over. And he never has, but . . . never again.

Dear Diary,

Have you ever heard of a movie called Baraka? Probably not. I hadn't. And when Aurelia said we were going to see it, at first I thought she said Barack, as in President Barack Obama, and I asked her how she knew him.

She didn't know what I was talking about. So I asked her again. About Barack Obama.

And she said, Baraka. Buh-RAH-kuh. It's a movie, and, Diary, you should see it. Not like you can, but if you were real—I mean, you're real because you're here with me, but I'm saying real like a person—then I would say you should definitely see it. I saw it today. Aurelia took me on a field trip to the movies. She said it was for history *and* science class.

We drove across town to this old movie place. At least it looked old. But Aurelia kept trying to explain to me that it wasn't really old but it sometimes showed old movies.

We ordered popcorn, gummy bears, gummy worms, Swedish fish (which are also gummy), and nachos. And water, because like Aurelia always says, health is wealth. We carried everything into the theater—thankfully, we were the only people there— and plopped down right in the middle of it all. Aurelia did that thing where you pretend like your head is blowing up and you make the *brrrrggghsssh* sound, and told me to get ready.

Ready for what?

That's what I was thinking as the movie started. There was some kind of flute playing, long, drawnout notes. *Fluuuuute. Fluuuute.* Mountain range. Big and beautiful and stone. And then from there we see a monkey in a hot tub. I know this probably all sounds silly, but if you saw it, you would be like, *look at that monkey in that water*, and you wouldn't be able to turn away, with all that *fluute, fluuute* going on in the background, and that monkey just sitting there, up to his neck in a bath, relaxing, looking at the camera. And I'm sitting there wondering where that monkey is, and where they have hot tubs made by God like that. And then . . .

Everything everywhere.

People, running and dancing and crying and

working and walking and spinning and moving and moving.

Animals, climbing and fighting and dying and running and swinging and moving and moving.

Things, like cars and buses and clocks and sun and moon, ticking and changing and swerving and crashing and moving and moving.

And *fluuuuuuute* was met with *boom boom boom* and *tap tap* and symphony and drums and so much more that I really can't explain. I guess the best way to explain it to you, Diary, is this is what you will be like when I've filled up all your pages, maybe. Or maybe if everyone—the whole world—wrote in you at the same time. Or something. I can't explain it right, but *Baraka* must mean something like *Whoa*. Either *Whoa*, or maybe it's the sound tears make but not the ones that come out, the ones that stay in. Yeah, that might be *Baraka*. Because that's how I felt at the end of it. Like maybe I should cry. But I didn't. But I felt like maybe I should. And, honestly, I didn't even really know why.

As the credits rolled, Aurelia exhaled as if she'd been holding her breath the whole time, and asked me what I thought.

I hadn't even touched the popcorn. Or the nachos.

Or any of the gummy stuff.

I told her I didn't know.

Then she asked me what I thought it was about.

I told her I didn't know that, either, but that at the same time I did know but didn't think I knew.

Aurelia said what she thought, which was, everything is moving. Everything. Even the things that aren't are, because the world is moving. It's spinning, so everything is changing constantly. Her, me, Darryl, and even you. And that somehow everything is still connected. Aurelia gets deep like Coach sometimes too. And I like it.

Dear Diary,

Practice was funny. Sort of. The part of it where I tried to explain *Baraka* to Patty while we were stretching. That was funny.

I told her the movie was deep. Deeper than deep.

Stretch.

She couldn't believe there were no words. Stretchh.

I told her, over and over again, that it was just action. Stretchhh.

And Patty didn't get it. But Lu said he did.

He said there would be all action whenever a movie was made about him. Stretchhhh.

And then Aaron jumped in all huff and puff and blow your house down. He said no one would ever make a movie about Lu. Then, switch!

Lu said they'd make one about him before they'd make one about Aaron. Sounds true.

Ghost said, Womp womp.

Patty laughed. I laughed. Then Aaron said something about me not being allowed to laugh because they were having a runners' conversation.

And then I was gonna tell him that I didn't know there was a such thing as a runners' conversation, but before I could, Lu said he was right. And that I was not a runner no more. That I'm a thrower. Then Lu said he was a thrower too. He put his fists up and said he had those two things to throw right at Aaron's face.

Patty made that weird noise when you blow air out your nose in a short burst as a way to be like, ohhh. The noise that sounds like gkish. Ghost nodded and held his fists up too, and then, of course, Coach came over and said those hands better be getting ready to work on form. Then he told Lu to count us off. Not Aaron. Lu.

Ghost said womp womp again.

I should've just named it Womp Womp Wednesday because while everyone else ran ladders, which would've been a piece of cake for me—to run four laps, then three, then two, then one, then one, then two, then three, then four, which comes to five miles—I had to spin around the track. Like . . . spin. Around. The track.

Coach said the plan was to work on the second spin. The second *whoosh* in the *whoosh whoosh.*

This picks up where the rules for the first whoosh left off.

6. Then go straight into a 180-degree turn, completing the second *whoosh*.

But the way he wanted me to practice it was to line up on one of the white lines on the track. The lines that make the track lanes. One of the ones on the outside, so that I'd be out of the way. Coach told me to keep my feet on the line. That every step—after the 230, then after the 180—should land on the line. Coach demonstrated it so I could see how it was done. Then he did it again. Then again. Faster. It looked silly when he did it slow-motion, but once he sped it up, it looked almost like the way a ballerina would walk down the street if they didn't want to just walk regular, and maybe wanted to show off. Just quickly spinning and prancing—Aurelia calls this allegro—which I think is sort of beautiful.

Spin, step. Spin-step.
Spin, step. Spin-step.
Coach told me it was just like ballet. I asked him if he knew ballet.

He said he didn't.
I told him I did. And that he was close.

Dear Diary,

On the way home, I tried to explain *Baraka* to Darryl. He also thought I was talking about the president, and when he found out I wasn't, he laughed. Just a little. But that little laugh led to me talking about the monkey in the bathtub, and the monkey in the bathtub got us through traffic, through all the people trying to get home, and I talked about all the people in the movie running and dancing and crying and working and walking and spinning and moving and moving, and then we were getting out of the car, going into the house, where we heated up TV dinners that were supposed to be meat loaf but Darryl called it "some animal," and I explained the animals in *Baraka*, climbing and fighting and dying and running and swinging and moving and moving, and then we were in the family room, standing at the big table where the puzzle pieces were scattered and just my mother's eyes—Darryl completed them last night on his own—stared up at us, attached to nothing, like random spots of dark and light, and I told Darryl about the cars and buses and clocks and sun and moon, ticking and changing and swerving and crashing and moving and moving. And *fluuuuuuute*. *Fluuuuuuute*. A sound that sounds both sad and happy. And that sad and happy made me bring up why I quit running.

I asked Darryl how come he never asked me about it when it first happened.

He said he asked me about it last night. But then Mr. Nico came.

And I said he said Gramps asked him to ask me.

And he said Gramps did ask him to ask me.

And I asked why didn't he just ask me.

He asked me what there was to ask.

I told him he could just ask why I did it.

So he did. Just asked. Just asked it while helping me piece my mother's cheek together.

And I told him. Well, I didn't just tell him. First I counted to ten. I don't know why, after all that buildup. I guess I was trying to figure out the best way to say it. One, two, three, four, five, six, seven, eight, nine, ten. And then . . .

Diary, I'm going to try to tell you how it went, but I might get some parts wrong. But I'm going to try anyway. This is how it went.

*I hate running the mile.*

*What do you mean, you hate running the mile?*

*I hate running it. I never liked it.*

*But you've been running the mile for so long. And you're so good at it.*

*Because you made me.* That's not what I said. Not yet. I said,

*I know I'm good at it but*

*You're not just good at it. You're the best. First place.*

*Your mother*

*I know my mother would be proud. I know I'm doing it for her, but what about me?*

*What about her? She didn't get to do this. To run her race, Sunny.*

*But but but*

And then I started counting again. One, two, three, four, five, six, seven, eight, nine, ten. And then . . .

*But when do I get to run MY race?*

I pushed the bottom of my mother's jaw into place, and judging by the shading of black and brown and gold, I could tell her cheek was lifted. She was smiling. I was not.

Then came the *boomtick*. But not with dance, with words. The stuff I usually write in you came out and flew right at him. And this time, I told him everything.

*I don't like running, I like dancing.*

*Running is boring, and nobody even pays attention to the mile, and you never asked me if I liked it, never even asked me. Never asked me what I do like, or if there's anything else I want to try. Never noticed my brown face blue and grey like business suits. With one leg too long. As long as I kept winning, right?*

*And even when I do, you tell me it's not good enough. My form was this, my stride was that, my breathing is off, breathe, Sunny. Breathe. That's what you say? You say I have to breathe, but I can't. I can't breathe. I can't breathe.*

Dear Diary,

*Boom tick tick tickboom* don't mean shoulder shrugs and robotic moves and tippy-toe to heel . . . things. It don't mean an explosion of dance. At least not for Darryl. But it does mean an explosion. An explosion that begins with a vibration. Darryl's body shaking like you shake, Diary, when the wind hits your pages. Shaking like you might rip out and fly away. Darryl's jaw was jumping, and he bit down on his own mouth to trap the cat in, I think. He kept nodding at me as we stood on opposite sides of the big table, nodding like he heard me, nodding like he heard someone else whispering to him. The nod turned into a bow. Him, folding in half.

I asked him if he was okay, and he just nodded. Then he bent over, his puzzled face kissing my mother's puzzled cheek, then swiped the puzzle box off the table. All the peace, but none of the pieces.

Darryl apologized, his voice, eeeee-ing like a creaky door. Like a house settling. Then he told me to go to bed.

So, I said night.

# 7

# THURSDAY

Dear Diary,

You know how I always say I was born in the middle of a hurricane? Well, that's true. But I realised last night that maybe I was born in the middle of two. And this morning felt like a third.

It started the usual way Thursdays start. No, it didn't. It didn't start the usual way at all. Aurelia was late. My father was already gone to work by the time the doorbell rang, and when I opened it, there she was, holding a paper bag with our sausage sandwiches in it.

She said there had been an accident, and as soon as she said it I thought about Patty's aunt, who got in a car accident a few weeks ago, and that scared me, but then I knew nothing was wrong because Aurelia was standing in front of me with her arms and legs and head connected to her body, so I knew she was okay. And because of that, I went from being all the way scared to all the way happy, and wrapped myself around her and squeezed tight.

Aurelia is like my best friend. I don't need her to ever be accidented. Ever.

Then she said she wasn't in an accident, somebody else was, but that it was just a fender bender and everybody was being nosy and we'd better hurry up and eat so we can get going.

Diary, the sausage sandwiches were cold. We warmed them up and that made them hot, but also hard. But I had to eat, and I didn't want to seem ungrateful because Aurelia bought them for us, so I started choking mine down, and then I actually choked, mid choke-down. A chunk of bread that had scientifically become a stone in the microwave got stuck in my throat. And well, I started to panic.

There are things that happen when you panic, especially when you're choking. Things I never knew. I had never choked before. The first thing you do is think you're going to die. That's also the second thing you do. And then you start pointing at yourself. It's weird. Every time I see someone choke in the movies, the people they're with never seem to notice, and I always thought that was fake, until it happened to me. Aurelia was sitting right in front of me, looking right in my face, and she couldn't tell I was choking and thinking about dying and thinking about dying again, until I pointed to myself. To my mouth and throat. And then the guessing game began.

Sunny?

Then, You choking? (*Ding ding ding!* Correctamundo, on the first try!)

*I'm choking!* I yelled in my head, but it just sounded like *cack, cack, kech, krrr, krrr,* all of which are basically the word "choke" without the vowel sounds. That's what choking does. It eliminates vowels. I realised that, too.

Then Aurelia jumped up, and screamed what we both already knew.

You're choking!

Now, this is the part that I didn't expect. No one really knows what to do. Not me. Not Aurelia. Not even you, Diary. So I did the first thing I could think of, and no, it wasn't dance.

I just started throwing things. Not, like, really throwing things, but knocking things around. I spun and swiped the rest of the breakfast off the island, even Aurelia's, then I staggered backward and knocked the washing-up liquid and paper towels and basically everything on the counter onto the kitchen floor. I don't know why. Just a reaction. When you choking, you just have to move. Can't just stay still when there's a chewable but not-so-chewable golf ball stuck in your throat, cutting your air.

Aurelia also didn't know what to do, so she ran over to me and told me to turn around and started beating on my back, which, let me tell you, doesn't work. Then she threw her arms around me, grabbed me around my stomach and just started yanking me and pulling me toward her, which I guess was supposed to be the Heimlich maneuver. And she did that for a while, and I kept hacking and hacking, and eventually, guess what? It didn't come up. It just went down.

That was breakfast.

That's how the day started. With me almost choking to death on a hot piece of a too-hard bread. And after I got over how scary it was, we laughed about it.

It can only go up from here.

Dear Diary,

I'm sure you could probably guess that me and Aurelia were late to the hospital. When we finally got there, Gramps was in the lobby already. But he wasn't waiting for us, he was talking to Patty's aunt. The same aunt I had just been thinking about when Aurelia came to the door talking about car accidents. Now, Diary, I don't know if this is true, but I might be one of those special people who make things happen by thinking about them. So I'm going to try to remember to think about throwing the discus on Saturday morning. I'm going to imagine myself throwing it a long, long way. I'm also going to imagine my father laughing. And I'm going to do that right now. Anyway, Patty's aunt was talking to my grandfather and telling him something about how hard it's been for her to depend on other people since she broke her arm, and how Patty is doing the best she can, but she doesn't want to distract Patty from school and running.

Then Gramps introduced me to her, and before she could say anything, I just gave her a hug because I had just been thinking about her, which now that I think about it, might've been weird. Even weirder than a wave.

I also didn't think about how a hug could hurt. Especially when your arm's broken.

I apologised, and I told her that I only hugged her because I know her. From practice. And that I was Sunny.

Guess what, Diary? She called me a celebrity! And said she'd heard a lot about me and how I was going to be the first thrower for the Defenders. I told her that was true but that I might not be as good a thrower as I am was a runner.

And she said she thinks I can throw the discus a mile. Maybe even two.

Diary, I wanted to tell her that was impossible, but she was so nice and she already had a broken arm, and I'd already almost died, so I felt like maybe we should let some of the small things slide. She thanked my grandfather again, then told me she'd tell Patty she saw me. And once she went to catch her ride, Gramps asked me and Aurelia what took us so long.

Aurelia told him it was a long story and that it didn't matter because we were there and we were ready. But Gramps didn't look good. He looked like something was happening behind his skin. Like his thoughts were making his stomach hurt. Like they were milk that had become glue in his gut.

Dear Diary,

~~I know I said a little while ago that my day can only go up from here but~~

Like I said, Mr. Rufus deserves his own entry.

There's something weird that happens when your grandfather, who is a doctor, tells you your favorite patient of his *took a turn*. "Took a turn" doesn't mean what it means on the track when you take the turn. It doesn't mean what it means when you're doing a puzzle and you take a turn to put a piece in. It means upside down. It means not good. It means stuff like amniotic embolism, or, in Mr. Rufus's case, coma.

There's something weird that happens when you hear, *He's fighting for his life*. There's a feeling that comes over you, that came over me, that sounded like, *Cushhhhhh*. The same sound of a crowd going wild or a TV on a bad channel. I felt like a TV on a bad channel. Like I didn't have a signal and couldn't get a clear picture. It's weird for nothing to be a feeling. The feeling of nothing is still a thing. And it sounds like *Cushhhh,* and it feels like falling in slow motion.

But I was somehow able to say, in regular motion, that I wanted to go see him.

Mr. Rufus changed overnight. Like, even though he's just in a deep sleep—a deep sleep he might never wake up from—his face looked completely different. I can't really say if he looked like he had become older all of a sudden, or if he maybe went backward and became an infant again. I don't know, but it kind of seemed like both.

Gramps said that there was no point in us doing our dance routine because Mr. Rufus wouldn't be able to see us, but that if I wanted to talk to him, he could hear me.

So I sat next to his bed. I didn't really know what to say to him. I mean, I only know him from coming to the hospital twice a week and dancing for him. But he's the one who always danced with us. He always bopped around in the bed and laughed and it was kinda like he understood me, just by doing that. I figured I could share whatever was on my mind. I mean, I didn't know what else to really talk about. So I leaned over and whispered in his ear and told him I almost choked to death this morning.

Gramps said, what?! And almost freaked out, but then caught himself and told me to keep going. And I explained how weird it was, and how I couldn't breathe and I couldn't speak and I was scared, so I pretty much wrecked everything around me. And I told him how Aurelia was sitting right in front of me, and she couldn't tell I was choking. How she was looking right at me. I admitted that I didn't know why I was telling him this and that I guessed I just needed to tell someone how scared I was. Then I switched up on him and told him my birthday was on Saturday. And as soon as I said that, I thought about how maybe that's not a good thing to talk about while Mr. Rufus is in a coma. So I stopped there. Because, Diary, I could feel myself Diarrhea-ing. So I paused. Just gathered my thoughts, which you know is sometimes hard for me to do because they are all over my head. Some are in the back and some are in the front and some are tucked just behind my ears, and others pressing hard against my eyes. And a few, I think, are at the tip-top of my head.

Thoughts that want to sprout out and be like antennas or something like that—maybe they would find a signal to clear up the picture—and I thought about telling Rufus all this, but then I thought maybe Rufus would like to hear about something more... interesting.

*Baraka*. I asked him if he'd ever seen it. Then I told him, not  Barack Obama. Buh-RAH-kuh. I told him it doesn't have words or actors or nothing like that, but it's still pretty good. I told him Aurelia thinks it's about everything. That we're all moving. Even when we're not moving. I told him that was the good news. That he's still moving.

When I finished telling Mr. Rufus about how much I hoped he could see Baraka once he got out of his coma, and to not spend money on popcorn and nachos and gummy things because he wouldn't even be able to eat them, Gramps asked if there was anything else I wanted to say.

And then it hit me.

He could hear me. I know, I think, every move, every action, has a sound. Has a tick or a boom. Or something. So I did the dance routine, without the music, without the moves, but with the sound. And I ended with attitude. My kind of attitude. Mr. Rufus's kind of attitude.

Not, *What!*

But, *Wow!*

Dear Diary,

Because me and Aurelia were so late, most of our regular dance appointments were already getting their treatments or being visited by family, so we couldn't catch everyone. Mr. MacAfee was already deep into nap time, so we decided to just leave. But before we did, Gramps wanted us to come back to his office.

He said he had something for me.

When we got there, he opened a drawer and pulled out a folder, and in that folder was a copy of a photo.

Aurelia leaned over my shoulder to see it.

My mother. It looked like she was at a party, maybe a barbecue or something. The picture was mostly a blur because she was in motion. But her face was clear. Gramps pointed to what looked like a whoosh of wind, which was apparently a bulging belly, and said that was me.

Aurelia said she remembered the day it was taken.

That it was during the baby shower. *Your mother was about to pop.*

Gramps said, if he recalls correctly, this was a few days before I was born. He said it might even be this exact day, but back then.

And Aurelia covered her mouth. Which meant it was probably true. She went on about how my mother didn't want a normal thing with gifts and games and all that. That she wanted to have a party. A real party. She wanted to dance, even though she could barely move because of her belly. Aurelia said my mother wanted me to know what happiness felt like, no matter what, from the inside out.

I stared at the photo. Her face. My face in hers. My body in hers. *Baraka*, all over again, the tears pushing against the backs of my eyes, my thoughts interrupted by Aurelia's sniff sniff sniffle.

Aurelia said she was sorry.

I told her it was okay.

Gramps told me to give the picture to my father. He said there are certain things he can't tell him. Certain things only she can.

Dear Diary,

Practice was weird because I showed up with a photograph folded and stuffed in my sock, and a million things on my mind. Choking. Mr. Rufus. My mother. I tried to push everything back back back, into the boot of my head as we all stretched (on Lu's count). Toe touches, high knees, star jumps, some other kind of toe touches, a different kind of high knee, some arm stretches, right, then left, then right, then . . . everybody left me. As in, left the track. It was Thursday, and Thursdays used to basically be Sunny Days because they were always my time to shine. This was our long run practice. The practice to show and improve endurance. And endurance is my specialty. But now, because I don't run anymore, the rest of my team broke out without me, Whit leading the way while I stood on the field. By myself. Not totally by myself. Coach was there. But still.

Coach brought over a milk crate full of discuses, clanging around like caveman plates. And while he was waddling from the weight of them, he yelled out that today was the day.

Today . . . is . . . the . . . *day!*

Coach dropped the crate. He pulled one of the discuses out. Flipped it in his hand, then handed it to me. Then he grabbed another for himself.

Diary, holding a discus *should* be like holding a Frisbee, but it's not. Not at all. And that was a surprise. But it's actually like holding … um … actually, I've never held anything like it before. You have to lay it flat in your hand, and just let your fingertips barely grip it. Not a real grip. Just a tip grip.

Coach demonstrated how to hold it, and I tried to copy but it felt like the discus was going to slip out of my hand.

Coach said I have to trust it. Said I have to know that it will move with me.

Coach held it in his palm, then wound his torso, flipping his hand over so that the discus was on the underside, and when he brought his body back around he flipped his palm back up. He repeated this over and over again. Then told me to try, but this time try it with trust.

It all felt so strange, and it got stranger as soon as I brought it back, because it slipped out of my hand and almost dropped on Coach's foot, but he moved just in time.

I was embarrassed and scared for Coach's toes, but he was cool about it and just told me not to ruin his dancing career.

I tried again, and again, bringing it back and forth, following Coach's lead. He told me to spread my legs a little more, to open my stance and drop my butt down some, to *sit on the invisible stool*. Eventually it started to feel better. Back and forth, swinging my arms, swinging the discus, winding it up.

Coach reminded me that the discus was all about technique. He said that even though it's heavy, it's not about strength, it's about movement. He said to consider this the third part of our very unique dance routine, which would be the seventh rule.

7. Release.

Dear Diary,

It's best to have these in one place.

STEPS TO A *WHOOSH WHOOSH AHH* (for optimal discus throwing):

1. Stand straight, bend knees just a little.
2. Spread arms like wings.
3. Wind body back and forth with hands straight and stiff, cutting the air.
4. Count to three.
5. On three, spin right leg 230 degrees around.
6. Then go straight into a 180-degree turn, completing the second whoosh.
7. Release.

Dear Diary,

Did you know that you don't actually throw a discus? Right. What you do is *push it*. Yes, push it. And the funny thing about that is, Coach kept saying it should feel natural. But how?

I mean, the spinning feels natural. And Coach said if I'm spinning right, the discus will just move with me even though I'm barely holding it. But then . . . I'm supposed to push it off my first finger, instead of letting it fly off the back of my hand.

Coach demonstrated this. The first time he did it at half speed, and the discus didn't go too far.

Then he did it again, this time full speed, and the discus still didn't go that far. I mean, it didn't go like a mile or nothing. But it went. It definitely went.

Again. This time the discus flew flatter and farther.

Then it was my turn. And, Diary, let's just say it didn't go so well.

Turns out, throwing a discus is like . . . it's like nothing else. All I know is I was terrible at it. It was flying to the left and to the right, and when it was actually going straight, it was wobbly and clunky.

Coach said to do it again. To trust it. To trust me. So, I did it again.

Again. I did it again, again.

Again. Again, after the second again, each time different than the last, my index finger rubbing raw from the steel. It was all feeling weird, which somehow felt not weird for me, if that makes sense.

Until everyone started trickling back onto the track from the long run. Lynn came in first, Coach Whit running alongside her. Then came Curron and Freddy, and Patty and Krystal and Deja and Ghost and Lu and everyone else.

Coach told them to stay off the track, shooing everybody over to the benches. Then he turned back toward me. Told me to remember it's like dancing. A fluid movement. And that he could tell I was thinking about it too much.

I took a deep breath. Wound up again, holding another one of the cold plates in my hand.

Lu yelled out, Let's go, Sunny! And gave me a few claps. I could hear all the teeth sucking from all the way over there, probably because everyone figured he was just sucking up to take Aaron's spot as captain of the team. Either way, I appreciated it. I wound up again, back and forth, back and forth, bending my knees and settling into my stance, and after the fourth wind, I tore into my spin, once, then twice, and then I let the discus go. And it went. And it was perfectly flat, spinning like a record.

Headed right for the rest of the team.

Coach yelled for everyone to look out. They scattered, and, Diary, I'm so glad they did, because the discus smashed into the wooden bench, cracking it, knocking it over.

Curron barked my name.

Lynn stood beside him, looking at me with mean eyes.

It was just like the race. Just like when I pulled up. The looks on their faces of surprise and disappointment, like I had done something wrong. Like something was wrong with me. Like I didn't belong at the only place . . . I belonged.

Dear Diary,

If anyone ever calls you Journal because you look like one and they want you to be one, or if your spiral backbone spins out again and you've come all loose and they mistake you for trash, or think you're unusable, I hope I have the courage to do for you what Lu, Ghost, and Patty did for me.

Threaten their fingers until they call you by your name.

Dear Diary,

After the newbies got everybody off my back, and Coach gave his usual knock-it-offs and cut-it-outs, followed by his end-of-practice pep talk about how the best never rest, he hit me with a surprise.

I have practice tomorrow.

Coach said that even though tomorrow's Friday, I need the extra day of practice to at least make sure I can get the discus out of my hand in a way that won't put people in danger.

So yeah. That's happening.

Dear Diary,

You know how I describe the face Darryl sometimes makes? The stone turning into more stone? Well, today his face was more of the melty face, and the stone, instead, seemed to fill up all the space between us. And I could tell that both of us had thoughts going boing boing in our brains

boing boing in my brain like a
jumping bean,
boing boing in his brain like a
jumping bean
our brains a bouncy castle at a party we
want to invite each other to.

And as we pulled into the driveway, Darryl sent me his version of an invitation.

He said he was going out with Mr. Nico's sister tonight. Ms. Linda.

That's a good thing. Finally. And finally Darryl also said—and this is the invitation part—that he was sorry about last night. And I knew what he meant.

Dear Diary,

Darryl's gone out, and right now I'm sitting on the floor in my room. I've been sitting here for a while now. I know I already asked you this, but I just have to ask again. Do you know what it feels like to feel like a murderer? I do. Do you know what it's like for something to be wrong with you. To be born incorrect. To be born a hurricane. I do. I've been thinking about my mother all day. Since Gramps gave me the picture in his office. Since I stuffed it in my sock, it scratching me with every discus throw. I forgot to take it out and give it to Darryl when we got home. Forgot until I peeled my socks off and discovered it stuck to my sweaty ankle. Now I'm looking at it. And thinking about her more. I've also been thinking about choking, about not being able to breathe, and about Mr. Rufus. About everything. But mostly her. Thinking about her dancing, and who she was and who I am and who we could've been together. Wondering how things would've been different if she was here. Would I have ever been a runner? Would I have ever been a dancer? Would I be me? Maybe a different me. A me with more mother. That's for sure.

I should stop here, I think. I should.

Dear Diary,

I'm still awake. Second night in a row that I can't sleep. There are no sounds. Nothing is settling. I need to move. And maybe . . .
I don't know.

Dear Mum,

I have never ever said, Mum. Not out loud. I've never called anyone that. I've never even called you that and you are my mum. You were. You would've been. And you would've called me son. Sun. Sunny. Or maybe Buddy, or Peanut, or Waffle like Patty calls her little sister. And you would've smelled like pancakes. And we would've had a secret handshake and a secret language and a secret dance routine that we performed at Darryl's birthday parties because if you were here, Darryl would have birthday parties. If you were here, I would have birthday parties. You would probably be planning one right now. For Saturday. My birthday. And you would know that I would want you to throw me a surprise party.

Because you would know me.

You would know that I've never spoken on the phone to anyone my age. That I don't have anyone my age's phone numbers. That I've had teammates but never friends, until the Defenders, and even they don't know my birthday is Saturday. And on Saturday nights we would do something fun like eat pizza or watch movies or make up dance routines, and I would probably have to tell you that your dancing wasn't great, but that I could make it better, and help you get your booms and ticks right, and you would thank me. Not many people thank me for much, but you would thank me for that. And for helping you clean up the house. And for helping you do other things that I can't think of right now, but you would thank me, and I would thank you and then we would hug and you would smell like pancakes and we'd make pancakes and I would tell you how many pancakes Aurelia has had me eat over the years, which I think is over a thousand, and I'd have to lay back in the chair in the living room until my stomach stopped dancing to the fried batter batter, fried batter batter batter. But the chair wouldn't be there because it would be in your office so I would probably have to lay down on the floor, or beg Aurelia to take me to your office so you could fix me like everybody says mothers can, and I'd kick back and complain about my ROI, and how a stomachache isn't a good one, but that you wouldn't have quit, you wouldn't have given up on eating pancakes, or learning how to measure batter better. If only you hadn't given up on me.

On us.

I'm sorry. I don't mean that. I know you didn't.

Did you?

I hope you didn't. Of course not. Why would you give up on the plan? You wouldn't do that. You and Darryl had been planning everything since y'all were kids. Step by step to the finish line. But you pulled up early too. Plans change. Maybe I was the wrench in the plan. Have you ever heard that? Wrench in the plan. I can't be a wrench. Not hard enough. Not steel. And can't fit around nothing to loosen it up.

What else do I need you to know?

Aurelia is my best friend, which is cool because she was also your best friend. And best friends trust each other. And usually best friends have a lot in common, so sometimes when I'm with her, when we're in the car, I look over and pretend she's you. I pretend she's you turning the radio up, and bopping around in her seat.

I pretend she's you playing silly name games like Big Money Sunny, and stuff like that. But I know she's not. But I still pretend. Maybe you would have a bunch of stars tattooed on you. Maybe you'd have weird-colour hair and be the coolest therapist ever. And you would sit me down, and tell me to tell you what's wrong.

And I would say.

Dear Darryl,

~~Dad. Dad. Dad. Dad. Dad. Dad. Dad. Dad. Dad.~~
~~Dad. Dad. Dad. DAD DAD DAD DAD!~~
~~D A D! DADADADADADADADADADAD! dad.~~
You looked cool in your tan suit.

I hope you're having a good date with Ms. Linda. I hope she makes you smile a little. I think you deserve it.

Dear Darryl,

I wish. Stuff.

I wish stuff like a good job from you. And if you don't want to talk much, maybe just a hug. Maybe a kiss on the forehead like how I kissed my discus. But I'm not as cold or as hard. And neither are you.

I wish you knew that.

I wish you knew I know that.

And I wish I knew why you made me call you Darryl. And not Dad.

And I wish we weren't like statues with no arms. I wish we weren't like puzzles.

# 8

# FRIDAY

Dear Diary,

I have some news. Last night, after not being able to sleep, I got up and did something I've never done. Ever. I crept across the hall to Darryl's room. He wasn't home yet. I didn't just go in there for no reason. I went to put the picture Gramps gave me on his nightstand. That's all.

I pushed the door slowly open, slipped in, and closed it behind me.

I had never been in there. Not that I can remember. I only remember being in my own room. In my own space, my own crib, my own bed. My whole life. But now I was in his room. It was much cleaner than I thought, from what I could tell, minus the towers of stacked boxes of finished puzzles along the wall. In the dark,

I crept to the bed. Slid onto the side where the covers were already pulled back. Climbed in. Yanked the covers up to my chin. I laid on the left side. The side I figured he laid on.

I have to tell you something, and it's going to sound weird. But by now . . . you know.

I sniffed his pillow. Buried my nose in it and sniffed and sniffed. It smelled like nothing. Tried to know him. Tried to feel what it must be like to be him. To be here in this room, one-half of a whole plan, broken. One half of a person. Maybe. And then—and I don't know why I did this—I slid over. Slid over to what I guessed was her side. It was cold and the sheets were so flat, so stretched that they seemed hard. Like maybe bodies on cotton makes it softer or something. It was like resting my body on a thin sheet of ice, it shattering underneath my weight into water. I pulled the pillow from behind my head and while lying flat on my back, hugged it.

I sniffed it.

I imagined it smelled like something something maybe her.

It smelled like her.

Maybe her, I imagined.

And I started to cry. And sniff. And cry. And sniff. And bury my cry. And cry. And squeeze. And squeeze. And sniff. And cry. And squeeze. And squeeze. And then not bury my cry. And cry. And try. As hard as I could to swallow my howl. Squeezing the pillow. Tighter and tighter until I felt something on my skin. Something soft, like feathers. But not feathers. Too big to be feathers. Too . . . I don't know. I didn't know what it was, so I reached over and yanked the lamp chain, the room instantly warming with light. Then freezing once I realised what was happening. What was tickling me.

Not feathers.

Not feathers at all.

Ribbons.

First-place ribbons.

Years' worth of them.

I sat straight up in the bed and snatched the pillowcase off the pillow. The ends of it badly stitched together were bursting, ribbons pushing through like guts. My squeezing had caused the seams to come loose. I started yanking the ribbons out, years and years and years of them.

First place, first place, first place, long ones, short ones, first place, first place. And the whole time I'm still crying and now it's louder because I wasn't trying to swallow it anymore. And I'm pulling them out, and crying, and pulling and crying and suddenly Darryl opened the door. I didn't hear him come in the house, or walk up the steps or anything. He just appeared, just stood there in the doorway, staring at me covered in ribbons as if I had jumped in a pile of leaves.

First-place leaves.

He didn't say nothing. He didn't ask me what I was doing in his room. In his bed. He didn't ask me why I had destroyed the pillow. He didn't say a word. He just stood there. It was only when he came in that I even looked up long enough to see all the other pictures. The ones from their marriage, them kissing, them laughing, them in college, in high school, in middle school. Them, everywhere.

He was shaking as he slowly walked to the other side of the room, his eyes never leaving me. Then he sat on the edge of the bed, crawled into the midst of the mess I'd made, and hugged the rest of my tears out. He said he was sorry again,

but this time for everything
   *for what happened to your mother*
   *for making you run*
   *for running*
   *for shutting down*
in a voice that sounded like a sound I don't think I've ever heard. He said it over and over again, his arms wrapped around me, my eyes on the nightstand. We were two S's. SS, lying side by side. Ships, finally docked in the night.

Dear Diary,

You ever heard people say, things don't change overnight? Well, guess what?

They don't.

But at first I thought that they had. This morning I woke up in my father's bed, took a shower, got dressed, and went downstairs, and there Darryl was, pouring himself a cup of coffee.

He said he called Aurelia and told her to take the day off. And that he took the day off. And a few minutes later I kind of wanted to take the day off, and put the night back on, because me and Darryl were sitting in the kitchen ... just ... sitting.

Ummmmmm. Yeah.

Diary, I bet you thought we'd be as perfect as pancakes, but we were actually more like health bars. Made of weird stuff, just there to cut the hunger.

He said good morning. Then sipped coffee.

I said good morning. He asked if I slept well.

I told him I did. Asked him the same.

He said yes. Then sipped more coffee.

I asked if he maybe wanted pancakes.

He said sure. So I made pancakes. For six. And it was the first time I felt like stuffing pancakes in my mouth not to eat, but just to take the place of the cat that had my tongue. We ate in awkward. And suddenly, maybe on like bite number sixty or something, he pushed his coffee cup across the table to me. He never did that before. Never offered me coffee. So I figured I should take a sip. Diary, did you know coffee tastes like WHY IS ANYONE DRINKING THIS STUFF?!

Did you know that? Because that's what it tastes like. And when I took a sip, I couldn't even swallow it, it tasted so trash. But I couldn't just spit into the air either, so ... I just let it dribble back in Darryl's cup.

Oh no. I started to apologize, you know, rapid-fire sorrys like sorry sorry sorry sorry

sorrysorrysorry

sorry sorrrrry I'm so so so so so sorry

but before I could even get to "sorry" number five, Darryl had already hit his hundredth *HA!* He'd busted out laughing. Like, *laughing* laughing. I don't remember the last time I heard him laugh, and I definitely don't think I've ever heard him laugh that loud, and for that long.

It actually sounded kind of painful. Like a bad cough. Like hacking and hacking and hacking up something he'd been choking on for a long time.

Dear Diary,

I told Darryl about me choking on that sausage sandwich yesterday. There was even more laughter in his face, but he tried to hide it. But I laughed, and then he did.

I also told him about Mr. Rufus. That he was in a coma. Darryl didn't think that was funny. Which is a good thing, because it wasn't. Not at all.

I told him about me almost hitting my whole team with the discus. His laughter came back, but then he noticed that mine didn't, so he disappeared his immediately.

I told him that because of that, I had to go to practice today. He said he'd take me.

Then he told me a little bit about his date with Ms. Linda. Dinner. Told me she was nice, and smelled much better than Mr. Nico, who smells like he himself is a cigar. And that was all he said, and, Diary, I'm glad that's all he said, because the thing is, I'm glad he went out with her, but I don't want to know nothing else. He did say one other thing about the date, though. He said it made him feel younger. Like he had his *boomtick* booming and ticking again. (That part's me, not him. Darryl didn't say that.)

And that got us talking about my mother. And about when they were kids. He dug out a photo book and we flipped though old pictures of him with different haircuts, and my mother with different hair styles, and my grandfather with less grey hair, and Aurelia, who looked exactly the same. Darryl talked about how Gramps wanted him to be a doctor too. How he always said, saving a life is always more important than saving a pound. Darryl also talked about how my mother's parents died when she was in high school in a freak accident, and that Aurelia's family looked after her, which is why she looked after Aurelia when she got all messed up on drugs. Darryl went on and on about how him and my mum met on the school bus, and she used to cheat off his homework.

And on it went, the stories, each one better than the last, all of them making me feel like I was being warmed. I got to tell him more about the team. I didn't have much else to really talk about, because the team is the only part of my life that is not this house. Or Aurelia. The team is the *bada-bada-bangbang*. Is the zip and zap and what-what, so they are who I have to talk about.

I reminded him that Ghost was the one who jumped the gun.

And Lu is the albino one who looks like he's been to the Olympics already.

And Patty is the only girl in the crew.

Darryl thought the fact that I said crew was funny.

Then he asked me if I liked Patty.

I asked why he was asking.

He said because whenever I say her name, my face does a weird thing.

I asked what kind of weird thing.

Darryl smirked, then flipped through the photo album, back toward the beginning. One of the first pictures—a Polaroid of him and my mother at a Chinese restaurant. They were young. Close to my age. And scribbled on the border was, *D & R's first "date."* Darryl pointed to the image of him, pressed his finger on his own goofy photographed face.

And I could feel mine going all melty melty, *skwilurp bleep blurp squish.*

Dear Diary,

When we got to the track, Darryl got out of the car and walked over to the stands and took a seat in the exact spot he normally sits in during the meet. Coach was already there. When I think about it, Coach is always there. It's almost like he lives on the track. He's never late.

He shook Darryl's hand. Shook it long. Then told me to head to the track. Told me this was just like any other practice, so I needed to stretch and do warm-up laps. The usual.

I watched Coach and my father talk. I couldn't hear what they were saying because they stepped way back from the track. There was a lot of hand movement, and some arm folding, but ultimately it looked okay. After my two laps, Coach met me at the throwing circle. He had his crate of discuses just like the day before.

He said that all I was going to be doing was throwing. That's it. Just throwing to get me as comfortable as possible before the meet tomorrow.

Coach told me to keep my form tight, and to just *whoosh whoosh aah.*

And I went. Spinning and throwing, spinning and throwing, Coach standing beside me, feeding me the metal disks, making slight adjustments to my technique.

Coach would tell me to keep my knees bent.

He'd say not to muscle it, but to just let it leave my hand. To just let it go. And I was doing okay until one got away from me and shanked off to the right and landed on the track.

And then somebody yelled out something about how that could've hit them, and I turned around and it was Patty. She was strutting over to the track, and behind her was Lu and Ghost.

Coach yelled that this was a closed practice and that there was no riffraff allowed.

Then Lu called me riffraff and said if I'm here, they should all be allowed. That made me feel good.

Then Ghost spat sunflower seed shells and said we were like cockroaches and that where there's one, there's four. And I didn't know if that was true or not, but it's interesting to think about, and a little frightening.

Ghost had walked over after school, and Patty's friend Skunk—yep, Skunk—brought her and Lu.

Skunk, who unfortunately looks nothing like a Skunk, was over by the stands, shaking my father's hand.

They had come to support me. Lu said they knew I was used to leading the pack. Now the pack had come to help lead me. So now, with them watching, I started again with the spinning and releasing, the discuses sometimes chucking through the air wobbly, and other times cutting through the sky like a blade. And with each throw, whether good or bad, Lu,

Patty, and Ghost would cheer me on.

*Good one!*

Or, *Not bad!*

Or, *Don't worry about that one!*

Or, *Hey, as far as I'm concerned, that should be part of the field!*

And before I knew it, there was another voice. A deeper one. My father. He had come onto the track, onto the field and was standing off to the side, shouting.

*That's better!*

And, *Try again!*

And, *That's how you do it!*

And when all the discuses were thrown, they

all clapped for me like a bunch of weirdos. And helped me retrieve them all so that I could throw each discus again.

Diary, after a few rounds of that, I'm happy to say I was consistently getting the discus up in the air, flat and straight. It wasn't going into outer space or nothing, and it was definitely not going a mile, but it was flying. Coach spent the last thirty minutes of practice just nodding, which for him is always a good thing.

At the end of practice Coach told me he thought I was ready, and that I could at least place third because there's only three of us competing.

Patty didn't like that. She said I'm taking first, like always.

I didn't say nothing to that. Just smiled because it was cool that she believed in me like that. That they all did. But the truth is, I'm not sure I even really care about winning at all.

Dear Diary,

After all that throwing, I was starving, and for once was looking forward to getting home and snatching a TV dinner from the freezer, opening the box, poking holes in the plastic cover with a fork, then microwaving that thing into a steamy, weird-smelling meal. Yum. But Darryl had other plans.

He ended up taking me to the Chinese restaurant him and my mother went to on their first date, which happened to also be the same Chinese restaurant me and Lu and Ghost and Patty and Coach went to on our first date. Back when the season was just getting started and Coach was trying to get us newbies to bond. Back when we shared secrets, when I found out about Patty's mum, and Ghost's dad. And how Lu always wanted a brother. Back when I shared my own secret about my mother dying and being forced to run by the man who was now sitting in front of me, flipping through a Chinese food menu the same way he flips through the newspaper on Sundays.

When the waiter came over to take our orders, I let mine rip. Peking duck and a cherry Coke. And before the waiter could say they don't have cherry Coke, I told him that I knew they didn't have it so a Coke with a little cherry juice in it was fine.

Darryl just shook his head. He ordered sweet-and-sour chicken, and asked me where I learned about Peking duck.

I told him Aurelia orders it sometimes for lunch.

He nodded and said my mother used to order that too. Said it was one of her favorite dishes. That, and sausage sandwiches.

My cherry Coke came out. I took a sip. It was delicious. Diary, remind me to thank Patty tomorrow. Anyway, that first sip brought up an idea. Especially since I didn't really know what to talk to Darryl about. Besides random comments about chopsticks and my mother, things were pretty awkward, not in a bad way, but in a way that made me keep moving around on my side of the booth, trying to get comfortable on the sweaty vinyl.

So I did the only thing I could think of. I asked Darryl to tell me a secret.

Then I had to repeat the request.

And finally after saying, a secret, a secret, like ... a secret, he told me why he made me call him Darryl, and not Dad. He said he didn't feel like he could truly be a dad without my mother. And that it just didn't feel right. Like, I'm his son and he's my father, but she would never be able to hear me call her Mum, so he just felt like it was unfair for him to be called Dad. He also admitted that maybe that's not a good reason, but . . . it's the truth. I was supposed to be the biggest return. Hearing Mummy and Daddy was supposed to be the ultimate ROI. The greatest moment in their plan.

I asked him if he wanted me to call him Dad. He asked me if I wanted to.

I told him I didn't think so. Then asked him if that made him sad.

He asked me if I hated him. I said, of course not.

*Then Darryl is fine. Cool.*

*Now, your turn. Tell me a secret.*

At first I thought about telling him about you, Diary. About how I still talk to you through writing. And how really that's kinda weird, but I like it. I like you. But then I was like, no, that's not a big deal, not nearly as big of a secret as me talking to myself. Like having full-on conversations. And none of that's as big of a deal as me sometimes climbing into my baby crib, since it's still in my room. But I wasn't ready to talk about that yet. What I really wanted to say, what I really wanted to tell him was something new, something fresh that I was holding in.

I'm scared about tomorrow. About the track meet.

That's what I told him.

He asked why.

I told I'm used to running the mile, and knowing that I will win, and when I do, I know I've made my team proud, and made my mum proud. I knew I'd be putting that ribbon in his hand. But if for some reason tomorrow, I don't do well, then I've let everybody down. Him, the team . . . my mother. Everyone. Darryl set his fork down.

His face stoning up in that serious way. He told me that he knows he hasn't been the kind of father that gives advice but that he was going to give me some now. And then he said that when I step into that circle, and I do that weird spin, and I let that discus go, don't think about him, or the team, or even my mother. He told me to let it go for me.

Dear Diary,

After dinner we came home, and before going to bed, we stood over the big table in the family room, picking through the pieces left to the puzzle we were working on. The face was complete, and the tricky part was now getting the rest of her body done, but most of it seemed to be blurred, like wind. It was the picture. The one Gramps gave me. The baby shower. And as Darryl and I tried blurry piece after blurry piece until finally completing most of her torso, we didn't talk too much. Just worked together. And when we finally said good night, we did this weird hug thing like we had just grown arms, and before going upstairs, I glanced at the puzzle, at the blur, and knew I was in there.

# 9
# SATURDAY

Dear Diary,

I don't have time to say much this morning because it's meet day, and I'm too nervous to write anything except for maybe, I'm so nervous. Wish me luck.

Also, I hope Darryl is okay. Today is the day my mother died.

Dear Diary,

By the time I got downstairs, dressed in my Defenders uniform, ready to go to the meet, Darryl had already made breakfast. Pancakes and eggs. But I told him I can't eat. Too nervous. Actually, first I thanked him. Then I told him I can't eat because my stomach had been tied in knots all morning. Milky glue guts. So for the first time in forever I turned down pancakes.

Darryl said it was okay. Then he said Happy birthday.

Happy birthday. Usually my birthday is spent with Aurelia taking me to a dance show or a concert, always always always something experimental that involves face painting and neon lights, which is cool, but I'm not sure how much of that screams *Happy birthday, Sunny.* But I always appreciate it. It's more than anyone else usually does, and by anyone else, I mean Darryl. Darryl normally just takes this day off. Like, off of everything. He usually just sits in his chair and be stone.

Dear Diary,

Diary, I don't want to bore you with all the stuff about the ride to the track. Or even the track itself. It's always the same—a pretty quiet ride (quiet and cool, not quiet and weird) through the city, past the big inflatable purple long-armed monster dancing outside Everything Sports, eventually leading us to a track packed with people. So many people. Family members and friends stacked up in the stands, ready to cheer on their favourite runners. But I wasn't a runner no more. And as we turned into the parking lot, that fact slapped me in the face.

For the first time in my life, I wasn't going to run. Darryl asked if I was ready for this.

I told him I was.

But . . . the thing is, Diary . . . I wasn't ready. And when I got out of the car and started walking toward the track, I started thinking of a way out of it all. A new plan.

I. OPTION 1: APPROACH THE TRACK (don't turn back)

A. Warm up and stretch with everyone as if

nothing is wrong. You have the whole meet to figure out how to get out of this, because the discus is going to be the last event. If all else fails, just say it's your birthday and you'd rather throw a party than throw a discus, and that next week you'll be ready.

B. Run the mile as if you totally forgot you weren't running it no more.

C. Throw the discus and embarrass yourself.

II. OPTION 2: DON'T APPROACH THE TRACK

A. Cry.

B. Poop on yourself. (If crying doesn't work. But know, there's no coming back from this.)

C. Sunny . . .

*Sunny!*

Darryl was calling my name. I didn't even know I'd stopped walking. Sheesh.

I continued on, looking out at the field as I got closer to it and the track, the white lines like rings around a green planet. A planet I'm used to orbiting. But now I was supposed to be locked down. I was supposed to fling the tiny metal spaceship back into outer space. I wished it could take me with it.

I took my place on the track just outside of everyone else. I mean, I was close to Patty, Lu, and Ghost, but not in the mix like I normally would be. Just a little bit away from everyone. I don't know why. Just felt different, I guess. Then Coach revved up and dropped his pep talk on us. He said that we were there to defend four things. 1. Our reputation. 2. Our work ethic. 3. Our ability. And more importantly, especially this week since I was doing something new, we're defending 4. each other. Whit was standing next to him, nodding. Coach crossed his arms and Whit put hers behind her back. Then Coach said this is what it means to be a team. To be family. It means things change, but they keep moving. Coach probably didn't even know he was describing my new favourite movie.

Then Coach sideswiped everyone and told Lu to lead the stretches.

Not Aaron. Not Aaron. Not A A R O N. LUUUUUUUUUUUU!

Dear Diary,

Coach sees almost everything. And if he doesn't, Whit sees it. But for some reason no one saw Aaron push Lu after the stretches. Not even Patty. But I did. And I started walking over to Aaron to let him know that even though I always try to play it cool, I have some noise for him. But before I could get to him, Coach called me over and told me he had some news, and having news is what people like Coach and Gramps say before they say someone or something has taken a turn.

And things definitely took a turn.

*They rearranged the events because of this new field event. It's only three of you, so they've decided to put you all first.* That's what Coach said.

I felt like I was going to pass out. All my *tickboom* had turned into a sputter, and the glue feeling in my stomach had turned into something else. Something heavier.

Like a discus. But only until the balloons showed up.

It was Aurelia. And Gramps. They were climbing up into the stands with like a hundred balloons.

I just told Coach before he asked.

*Today's my birthday.*

Coach said, today? I said yeah.

He asked, why didn't I tell the team?

I shrugged.

Coach told me to hurry up and speak to my family.

We had work to do.

I ran off the track and gave Gramps and Aurelia hugs and they wished me happy birthday and asked if I was ready and all that, and I told them I was nervous and it felt like all those balloons were in my body. And that's when Aurelia pulled out a green marker, grabbed me by the wrist, and drew a star on my forearm. Where my mother's was.

For good luck.

When I got back to the benches, there were questions.

*Yo, Sunny, why you ain't tell us today was your birthday?*—Lu

*How you surprise your team with your birthday?*—Patty

*Anything else you want to tell us that we don't know?*—Ghost

*Um . . . I don't go to school.*—me

*You don't go to school! Who are you?*—Ghost again

*Be quiet, Ghost.*—Patty

*I mean, I do wanna know about this school thing, but right now we talking about your birthday. So, how come you didn't want us to know?*—Patty again. We were passing the Tupperware of orange slices— the ones from Lu's mum—around.

I told them that I just never really talk about it too much because I don't do that much to celebrate or nothing because it's also the day my mum died. And before they could make melty-sad faces, and do all the awful awww-ing, I told them it was fine. I was fine. And showed them the green star on my arm. None of them understood it—plus it was hideous— but . . . I knew.

Dear Diary,

The announcer made the announcement—
because that's what announcers do—that the
order of events had changed slightly, and that
there would be an add-on at the beginning of the
meet. The discus. He announced who would be
participating.

*And lastly, from the Defenders, formerly the master
of the mile, Sunnnnnnny Lancaster!*

It was time.

I walked out onto the track, and across it, onto
the grass over to the throwing circle. Coach came
behind me, a few discuses in his hand. Two other
throwers and their coaches were there swinging
their arms around, trying to loosen up. They
definitely looked a lot more relaxed than me.

Then the referee told us the rules.

If you go over the line or on the line, that's a
foul. If you step out of the circle, that's a foul.

If your discus goes outside the sector lines,
which means if it hits the track—foul.

We all nodded. And then the ref said
that because my last name, Lancaster, was
alphabetically before Watkins and Young, I was

up first.

Lucky Lucky Lancaster. Ugh.

Coach waved me over to where he was, which was just a few feet behind me. He put the first discus in my hand. He told me— reminded me—that I had this. That it was just like dancing. Whoosh. He told me to just let it flow, and let it go.

I stepped into the circle.

The sound of everyone watching . . . was silence.

I let the discus rest in my palm, let just the tips of my fingers grip it, just like we practiced. I wound, wound, wound, then . . . *spun, stepped, spun-step, THROW!*

*Foul! Stepped over the line, son.*

I tried to shake it off, and just grabbed another discus. Got back in position. Coach told me it was okay, and to settle down. Settle in. Coach bent his knees to demonstrate what he wanted me to do. Just like we practiced. Invisible chair. Sit in the invisible chair.

Darryl popped up just like he did a week ago when I quit. But his face wasn't stone. Or wax. And I wouldn't have even known if he didn't scream out, Let's go!

Aurelia popped up next to him.

Patty shouted, You got this, Sunny. You got this! And Lu and Ghost, and even Aaron and Lynn and Curron and Whit and . . .

Ease up, Sunny. Nice and easy. Again, I let the discus rest in my hand. Then, when I was ready, I wound, wound, wound, and whipped into my double-spin again, this time getting the discus off clean, spiraling through the air.

But hard to the right.

*Foul!*

The discus plinked onto the track, followed by the *ohhh* of the crowd. Coach ran over to me.

He said he could see it in my face.

I had no idea what he was talking about.

Coach explained that he could see . . . sound. In my face. In my body. He told me I needed to let it out. I needed to scream.

Diary, remember what I said about choking? When I had toast stuck in my throat blocking all my vowels? That's how I felt again. Like I should knock everything over, but there was nothing to knock over. Like I was panicking. This was my last chance. My heart was kicking a hole in my chest. *Boom-bap bap, buh-boomboom bap! Boom-bap bap, buh-boomboom bap!* And as I tried to settle it, tried to get it to quiet down, suddenly . . .

Sound.

A rumble coming from the audience like a storm approaching.

And I stared at the discus, and at that star scribbled on my arm in green marker, and wound...

*Boom-bap bap, buh-boomboom bap! Boom-bap bap, buh-boomboom bap!*

Everything is moving. Everything is changing.

Everything is connected.

And wound . . .

I am not a murderer. I am not a hurricane. Nothing is wrong with me.

*Boom-bap bap, buh-boomboom bap! Boom-bap bap, buh-boomboom bap!*

The sound tears make on the inside, I have to get on the outside. *Baraka*. I'm going to scream. Baraka. I'm going to scream it out and away. . . .

And, SPUN!

Turned. And

turned. And

let go.

# ACKNOWLEDGMENTS

Acknowledgments are interesting because I always feel like I'm thanking the same people. But that's because I've been fortunate enough to have consistent support. So . . . thank you Caitlyn, Elena, and Justin. You know how I feel about you all. Thank you, Mom. You definitely know how I feel about you. Thank you, Pop. Most people don't know how I feel about you, but soon they will. Thank you to the librarians, teachers, and booksellers. I hope by now you know how I feel about you. Thank you to my siblings, all of whom are kind of strange, but in the best possible way. And most of all, to the young people who read these books. If you've read this one—which I'm assuming you have if you're reading these words—hopefully your inner weirdo has been energized. We need your imaginative, courageous, unashamed selves now more than ever. THANK YOU.

# JASON REYNOLDS
## Author

Jason is a critically acclaimed writer and poet and the winner of more than 25 US and International awards including the 2018 Edgar Award, Newbery Honor, Printz Honor, and twice winner of the Walter Dean Myers Award. You can find his ramblings at JASONWRITESBOOKS.COM

# SELOM SUNU
## Illustrator

Selom is a devoted Christian working as a Character Designer and Illustrator. He currently lives in the UK with his wife and daughter. There are many sources of inspiration for Selom's work and he often thinks of the characteristics and features of family members when designing characters.

# ULTIMATE PANCAKE TOPPINGS

Sunny loves pancakes for breakfast! If you make pancakes, try some of these toppings:

**1. The Original:** maple syrup

**2. The American Classic:** bacon and syrup

**3. The PBJ:** peanut butter and jam

**4. The Sugar Fix:** chocolate chips and chocolate syrup

**5. The Fruity Freestyle:** blueberries, strawberries and cream

**6. The Banana Split:** sliced banana and chocolate syrup

# HELLO FROM KOHQ*!

Thanks for reading SUNNY.
We really hope you enjoyed it.

KNIGHTS OF is all about YOU. We make books for every kind of reader, from every kind of background and hope you'll read more of the great stories we publish. If it's fearless knights riding bikes or solving mysteries with your sister, if great stories are what you're after – we've got them!

Run to the next page to find out what the next book on the RUN series is.

*Knights Of Headquarters

**READ THE REST OF THE *RUN* SERIES:**

# GHOST
# PATINA
# LU

**WANT MORE BY
JASON REYNOLDS?**

**READ AN EXTRACT OF
*LOOK BOTH WAYS***

# LOOK BOTH WAYS

*New York Times* best selling author

# JASON REYNOLDS

# WATER BOGEY BEARS

THIS STORY was going to begin like all the best stories. With a school bus falling from the sky.

But no one saw it happen. No one heard anything. So instead, this story will begin like all the ... good ones.

With bogies.

"If you don't get all them nasty, half-baked goblins out your nose, I promise I'm not walking home with you. I'm not playin'."

Jasmine Jordan said this like she said most things—with her whole body. Like the words weren't just coming out of her mouth but were also rolling down her spine. She said it like she meant it.

Said it with the same *don't play* with me tone her mother used whenever she was trying to talk to Jasmine about something important for her "real life," and Jasmine turned the music up in her ears real loud to drown her mother out, and scroll on, scroll on. *If you don't take them earbugs ... earbuds ... airphones, or whatever they called out of your coconut head it's gonna be me turning up the volume and the bass, and I'm not talking about no music.*

That tone.

Jasmine's bogey-removal warning was aimed at her stuffy-nosed best friend, Terrence Jumper. TJ. Well, Jasmine called him her "best friend who's a boy," but she didn't have best friends who were girls, so TJ was her *best friend* best friend. And she was his. Been like that for a long time. Since he moved onto Marston Street, three houses down from her. Since the only way their mothers would let them be walkers was if they walked together because they were the only kids who lived on their block. Since six years, so since forever.

The bell rang, and Jasmine and TJ had just left their last class for the day, the only class they had together. Life science with Mr. Fantana.

"You been back to school for two days and you

already starting with me?" TJ spun the black lock dial confidently, like he could feel the difference in the grooves and would know when he landed on the right numbers.

"How could I not? Look at them things. Honestly, TJ, I don't even know how you're breathing right now," Jasmine continued. Their lockers were right next to each other, luckily, because Jasmine, unlike TJ, turned her lock with an intense concentration, glaring at it as if the combination could up and change at any second, or as if her fingers might stop working at any moment. And if for some strange reason either of those things happened, at least she knew TJ was right there to help.

TJ shrugged, tossing his science book onto the floor of the metal closet, the smell of feet wafting up from it like a cloud of dust, unsettled. And unsettling. The floor of his locker was littered with empty snack bags that Jasmine had slid through the door vent between classes over the last two days. Trash ... yes. But Jasmine and TJ called them "friendship flags." The litter of love. And because Jasmine had been gone for a while, they were basically notes that said *I've missed you*. In Cheeto dust.

Then, finally, with the hardened snot like tiny

stones rolled in front of the entrances of his nose, TJ turned the bottom of his shirt up and mopped it. A streak of slime smeared across his lip as he swiped and pinched and dug just enough for it to count as a dig, but not enough for it to count as *diggin'*.

TJ tilted his face upward so Jasmine could get a clear line of sight into his nostrils. *"Better?"* he asked, half sincere, half hoping there was one more bogey left and that it was somehow making a mean face at Jasmine.

Jasmine stared into TJ's nose like she was peering through a brown microscope of flesh, and she did this totally unfazed by the fact that TJ had just used his T-shirt—the one he was *wearing*—as a tissue. And why *would* she be bothered? Not that it wasn't disgusting (it was), but she'd known him a long time. Had seen him do things that made bogies on the bottom of a T-shirt seem like nothing more than added decoration. Bogey bedazzle. A little flavour for his fashion. Had seen him use his fingers to pick gum off the bottom of his sneakers (and hers), and of course nothing would ever beat the time he clapped a mosquito dead right when it had bitten him, then licked the fly slime off his arm. That one Jasmine had dared him to do. Paid him a dollar for it. Worth it, for both of them.

"Y'know, I can see straight through to your brain," Jasmine said, pretending to still be examining. "And it turns out, there's a whole lot of it missing." She plucked TJ's nose. "Sike, sike, sike, sike. Nah, you good. I guess I can be seen with you now."

"Whatever." Locker slam. "I mean, we all bogies anyway."

"*You* might be a bogey." Locker slam. "But me, I'm no bogey."

"That's what you think," TJ went on as they swapped backpacks. His was light. Jasmine's was packed with every class's textbook and all the world's notebooks. Makeup work. She could've carried it herself, but TJ was concerned about her back, about her muscles, because she was still recovering from the attack.

They headed down the crowded corridor, noisy with shoe squeaks and thick with end-of-day stink. "See, I've been thinking about this. Bogies aren't anything but water mixed with, like, dust and particles in the air and stuff like that—"

"How you know?" Jasmine interrupted. Knowing TJ, he could've heard this anywhere, like from Cynthia Sower—everybody called her Say-So—who jokes 99.99999 percent of the time.

"Looked it up online once," TJ explained. "Was trying to figure out why they so salty."

"Wait." Jasmine thrust a hand up, as if walling off the rest of TJ's words. "You eat them?"

"Come on, Jasmine. It isn't fair to hold my past against me. Dang." TJ shook his head. "Now, if you done interrupting, let me continue with my hypothesis." He broke "hypothesis" down into four fragmented words to put some spice on it. *High-Poth-Uh-Sis*. "So, bogies are basically water and dust." He put a finger in the air. "And human beings are mostly water, right? Isn't that what Fantana said at the beginning of the year?"

"Right."

"Okay, follow me. Every Sunday when we be at church, they always be talking about how God made us out of dust, right?" TJ and Jasmine went to the same church, where they sang in the youth choir together. TJ always asked Mrs. Bronson, the choir director, to let him sing solos even though his voice was all over the place. A set of wind chimes in a hurricane. And Jasmine's singing wasn't much better. Only difference was she knew it and would never think to ask for a solo. She loved to wear the "graduation" robes and harmonise and sway and clap, snuggling her voice into the others like drawer into dressing table. Her mother always told her, *Holding a note is talent enough.*

Even though TJ couldn't hold a note—that definitely wasn't his talent—he could hold a conversation. So he continued. "God making man from dust and blowing breath into his nostrils and all that, right?"

"I ... guess."

"You think God's breath stank?" "What?"

"Never mind. Probably not." TJ got himself back on track. "So, if God made man from dust, and now, for some reason, man—"

"And woman," Jasmine tacked on.

"Yeah, and woman ... consist of mostly water, then basically, we water *and* dust, right?" TJ was waving his hands around like he was drawing some grand equation on an invisible board. Jasmine didn't say nothing, and she didn't need to for TJ to bring his theory home. "Which means... ," TJ concluded, and Jasmine could practically see the drumroll behind his eyes, "we all basically ... bogies."